Escape from the Big Easy

Zombie Chaos Book 1

by

D.L. Martone

For Andy and Chris

We couldn't ask for two better brothers!

Chapter

1

"Good morning, Mr. Bassett. This is your wake-up call. Please move your ass." – Valentine McKee, *Tremors* (1990)

When I opened my eyes, I immediately spotted the axe – still embedded in the creature's skull. The ornamental stone weapon – which my wife, Clare, had given me as a Christmas present a few years before – had proven to be more than sufficient for hacking into a zombie's head.

Bet that was in the sales pitch at whichever French Quarter store she'd purchased it. Probably Marie Laveau's, our favorite voodoo shop.

It'll split a zombie skull open in one chop!

Somehow, I knew Clare would hate to see the black obsidian blade inches deep in zombie gore – blood and brain matter splattered along the carved wooden handle as well as the stones, hide, feathers, and fur that decorated it. On the other hand, she'd be grateful it had saved my life.

The lump on the back of my head throbbed as I stumbled to my feet. A patch of dried blood marked the lowest edge of the concrete steps leading into our rear apartment – likely the result of my noggin colliding with it. In fact, I'd struck it so hard I hadn't come to until morning.

Goose bumps dotted my forearms, no doubt thanks to lying outside all night. Rubbing my flesh to warm it up, I peeked around the left corner of the building, down the alley, to the blue, seven-foot-tall wooden gate that opened onto St. Ann Street. The path was clear of any other undead.

Luckily, I'd managed to close and lock the gate after the first zombie clawed his way into the alley. Though the creature had tripped and tumbled onto the ground, giving me a slight head start, I hadn't been able to escape him completely.

Scrambling to his feet, the disgusting thing had chased me toward the courtyard at the rear of the property. Before reaching our door, I'd experienced – in the dim glow of the patio lights – my first tussle with the undead.

It didn't exactly go as planned, but what ever does?

In the cold light of day, I realized the creature wore a pirate costume. I might've laughed if my head wasn't still throbbing.

Regardless, removing the weapon from his head was almost as tough as sinking it in had been. Every time I pulled on the handle, the entire body would rise, like the axe wasn't ready to relinquish its first kill. I anchored my foot against the zombie's face and pulled as hard as I could. The suction sound that resulted as I freed the blade almost made me puke. I didn't know what the dark putrid liquid oozing from his head was, but it didn't seem normal.

Of course, at this point, what the hell is normal?

A clang snapped me back to reality. I gazed toward the rotting fence that separated my courtyard from the one behind it and noticed the jiggling top of a ladder leaning against the other side.

Before the zombies came, it hadn't been uncommon for my rear neighbor, Tommy, a short, spry, seventy-two-year-old native New Orleanian to scurry up his ladder and, without notice or invitation, drop into our courtyard. He had a penchant for trimming our bougainvillea bush, a hardy, magenta-flowered vine that grew so well in the Big Easy's humid, subtropical climate, it often drooped over the fence and spread onto Tommy's property as well. Like most humans, it had no respect for boundaries.

I'd never minded my nosy neighbor's occasional disruptions because, frankly, I'd always despised that damn plant. Our landlord had put it there long before Clare and I rented our apartment, so my wife had never let me chop it down.

But every time one of us had ventured outside to trim the branches, we'd come back looking as if we'd just been attacked by an enormous, bloodthirsty porcupine. Why? Because beneath the gorgeous flowers lay a plethora of large hidden thorns that would often leave ugly scratches and bloody trails along our arms and legs.

So, whenever Tommy had decided to attack the bougainvillea with his big ol' clippers, I'd never tried to stop him. The trouble was... after climbing over the fence, he'd typically have no way of returning to his own courtyard – since Clare and I kept our ladder inside the apartment.

As a result, he'd simply exit via our front gate – which he'd always leave unlocked and wide-open. And nearly every time he'd done that, particularly when we weren't home, some drunken Bourbon Street reveler had inevitably found his or her way inside our alley.

Thanks to the zombie invasion, however, such an unwanted visitor could turn out to be an undead carnivore.

The ladder shuddered again, and I realized Tommy wasn't the one climbing it. A rail-thin Asian man, wearing a dirty white apron, slowly stepped up each rung. He resembled one of the cooks from Moon Wok, the Chinese restaurant on the corner of Dauphine and St. Ann. Of course, I couldn't be sure because at least half of his face was missing, and a useless eyeball dangled from his left socket, bouncing against his shredded cheek.

Given that I'd just woken up – with a head injury, no less – I still felt a bit dazed as he reached the second-highest rung on the ladder, his good eyeball fixed on me. He moaned and stretched his torso across the top of the fence separating our courtyard from Tommy's.

An instant later, the ladder slipped sideways, and he tumbled over the barrier, falling headfirst into one of our garbage cans, which in turn tipped over. Despite his obvious lack of coordination, he somehow managed to right himself, though most of his body remained inside the large plastic receptacle, rotten food and other bits of trash falling all around him.

While the former cook could no longer see me, he obviously still smelled me. Immediately, he charged in my direction and rammed my chest with his trash-can suit of armor. Stumbling backward, I tripped over the zombified pirate and landed squarely on my ass. The axe flew unhelpfully from my hand, and Sir Dead-a-Lot, who must've sensed I'd fallen on the ground, launched himself at me again.

Naturally, he also tripped over the dead zombie and promptly landed on top of me. Soon, I found myself hugging the round, unwieldy garbage can, straining to push it (and the creature it contained) off me. I saw the zombie's feet still moving and heard his frustrated groans, but fortunately, the creature couldn't reach me through the hard plastic.

Following an awkward struggle, I finally managed to propel the can off me, sending it in a haphazard roll toward the other side of the courtyard. The whirling motion must've loosened up the dangling eyeball because, beyond all odds, I watched as it jetted through the air and impaled itself on one of the bougainvillea thorns.

I mean, seriously, what are the odds?

The maneuver also had another unintended effect. As he'd revolved, the zombie must've gotten less wedged up inside the can, so once it came to a stop near the far wall, he grunted and began violently twitching, trying to wriggle himself free. I'd just scrambled to my feet and retrieved the axe when he finally popped out of the can. Either super-dizzy from his involuntary roll or simply stupefied due to his extreme undeadness, he took a moment to get to his knees. That gave me just enough time to cross the courtyard and, as he struggled to stand, plant the goo-stained axe blade into his head. Unlike my experience with the pirate, the blade slid easily from his skull as his body dropped motionless to the ground.

I leaned against the building, exhaling heavily, and glanced between the two zombies lying dead – or, rather, dead again – in my courtyard. Despite the dull ache invading my skull, I couldn't believe I'd almost been eaten by two zombies. Though not for the reasons you'd think.

For the previous fifteen days, I'd known the zombie infection would eventually reach New Orleans. If you'd followed my blog – and you were still alive, that is – what you thought were the crazy ramblings of some whack job had now become our shared reality. I hadn't started the blog to boast about my access to inside information; I thought it might actually help some people survive the epidemic. Foolish and naive, maybe, but true.

In my pre-zombie days, I'd never helped anyone whom I didn't love or at least like a whole lot. The blog had been my way of atoning for more than four decades of selfishness.

At least that's what I tell myself.

Naturally, I knew none of that would matter anymore. Soon enough, the blogs wouldn't exist at all. There would be no Internet, not one website. Hell, it wouldn't take long for the entire globe – or what remained of it – to lose its precious access to electricity, not just the billions of ridiculous sites that made up the World Wide Web. Civilization would disintegrate, if it hadn't already, and little would remain except the desire to survive at all costs.

Fittingly, the last-ever social media post would probably come from someone marking themselves safe... only to die after hitting *enter*.

As for me, I wasn't some conspiracy theorist with a ton of stolen data – or a government agent at the top of the pay scale. I was just a lowly entrepreneur, trying to avoid working for "the man," when I'd stumbled onto the truth.

My most recent home-grown business had involved creating smartphone apps. OK, I hadn't actually created anything. I'd merely come up with the ideas and planned out how the apps would work. Then, I'd have to find someone much brainier than I was to build them for me.

At first, I'd tried collaborating with a few college kids on the cheap, but that hadn't worked out so well. Incompetence was expensive at any price.

So, after much trial and error, I'd finally located the perfect guy for the job. As with so many businesses in the good ol' U S of A, I'd had to outsource the programming to India. Like most overseas contacts, Samir had begun our professional relationship as just an electronic employee, creating whatever weird apps popped into my head. Luckily (at least for me), he was extremely skilled at actualizing my ideas – and incredibly efficient, too.

After six months of successful releases, though, we'd gotten to know each other as more than mere colleagues. Initially, our friendship had emerged through emails and online chats, but it hadn't taken long before we started talking on the phone or via video calls. Even though we lived in two very different countries, with two exceedingly different cultures, we seemed to appreciate a lot of the same books, movies, and hobbies.

Our wives had similar interests as well – although Dibya, Samir's wife, had beaten us all when it came to brains and a career. Like Samir, she was a programmer, but while he and I had been developing an app to help people locate their vehicles in a mall parking lot (or something equally trivial), she'd been working for the United Nations to establish a network of satellites that would essentially provide free Internet access to the entire planet. Dibya was wicked smart: If not for her, we'd never have learned the undead would soon be a real-life dilemma.

In truth, most people had been rather skeptical of the I-World Initiative – the project she'd been a part of. They'd wondered how the U.N. could possibly provide free Internet access without any ground-based towers. Despite such criticism, the U.N. had approved – and fully funded – the program.

During a five-year period, the U.N. team had launched forty geo-synced satellites – and ultimately run into problem after problem. Satellites had lost power and become space junk. One had plummeted back to Earth, costing a whopping twenty billion dollars to replace.

By the time the U.N. team had discovered that almost half of the satellites were misaligned – meaning users would have to be in outer space to send and receive email – the public skepticism had turned to anger. People all around the world had labeled the I-World Initiative a complete failure, and the media (including all the late-night talk shows) had spent almost a month bashing it.

Then, while trying to remotely realign several of the satellites, Dibya had discovered a signal – well, there was no other way to say it – from "somewhere else." No matter where the mysterious signal originated, it had served as a warning to the human race: Earth was about to be invaded by creatures that, for lack of a better term, resembled the living dead. Worse, they'd bring with them a virus that would allow a zombie infection to radiate across the planet.

Dibya had done her best to spread the word – about the signal and its aftermath – but it was an uphill battle.

Don't you remember the day you initially heard the warning? The first time the media released the *oh-shit-we're-all-gonna-die!* message on national television?

That's right, you don't remember it – because the media never issued such a warning. Local, regional, and national government fucktards throughout the world never revealed the bad news. Difficult as it was to accept in the digital age, the powers-that-be had managed to clamp down and lock up any whispers of Armageddon.

Yep, great plan. What a bunch of asshats.

When the breach had occurred – and the infection, virus, or whatever it was started to spread – the whole damn mess had been covered up. As country after country went dark, those in the know had used every excuse they could. First, solar flares had been the supposed cause of any lost communication. Then, borders had been closed due to an advanced version of the Ebola virus. In fact, thanks to denial or ignorance or just plain selfishness, they had done everything possible to prevent the world from finding out... it was all coming to an end.

Chapter

2

"They're coming to get you, Barbara! There's one of them now!" – Johnny, *Night of the Living Dead* (1968)

Not long after having learned about the undead invasion, Samir and Dibya had virtually vanished off the face of the planet. Yet, the only reason I knew about any of it was thanks to Samir: Turned out the last app he'd prepared for me wasn't an app at all.

One afternoon, a couple weeks before the zombie wave hit New Orleans, a mysterious overnight package had arrived at the French Quarter Postal Emporium, where Clare and I kept a mailbox for our various business ventures. Labeled *URGENT* and addressed to *Joseph Daniels* (not one of our business names), the package contained a solitary flash drive – in itself an unusual occurrence since Samir normally uploaded the latest program to our shared cloud server.

Once I'd learned the truth, though, the puzzling flash drive made a whole lot of sense.

Following the breach and the ensuing epidemic, the powers-that-be had likely tracked Samir and Dibya's outgoing communications. Leaving snail mail as their last resort. And somehow, by the grace of someone, the package had reached us. Not snow, not rain, not heat, not even zombie invasions could thwart some couriers.

More than a little curious, I'd loaded the app onto my phone and entered the password Samir and I typically used for all our unreleased programs. But what was supposed to be our version of a white noise generator – to help people sleep or meditate or just calm the fuck down – had actually contained an audio message explaining everything that would happen.

As an unwelcome bonus, Samir and his wife were apparently in extreme danger and, consequently, wouldn't be able to contact me anymore. It saddened me to think I'd never talk to him again, but I also felt grateful he'd thought of me in his darkest days and managed to send me anything at all – much less classified information that had likely gotten him and Dibya killed.

Then, at the end of his message, came the kicker: I had only three weeks to get ready for the end.

However the epidemic had started, it had spread alarmingly fast – via direct bites or any other zombie fluids people managed to get into their systems. At first, the disease simply killed its hapless victims. Then, it animated the dead cells in any infected human bodies (with their brains still intact), effectively bringing recent corpses back to life as flesh-seeking monsters. Just like any good zombie flick, except without the benefit of make-believe.

All of those "chemical spills" that killed thousands across India had simply been the first dead zones. Incidents that, in the beginning, had been covered up by local and regional governments. When those entities could no longer handle the crisis, the task had moved to India's national administration. Every time the truth leaked out, the next level of fucking bureaucracy had done its best to put a lid on it.

In the end, I had far less than three weeks to prepare for the impending doom. Dibya's calculations on the probable distribution of the infection had missed the mark on that score, but sadly, the actual timing was the only thing Samir and his wife had gotten wrong.

So, I thought I had another six days to get out of Dodge. Well, the splattered blood, black ooze, and two zombie bodies on the pavement told me otherwise.

No doubt most people would've considered the whole mess one giant prank. I probably would've, too, but something about Samir's tone had made me a believer, even more so when I'd tried to contact him. As he'd predicted, that proved to be impossible. By the time I heard his message, he and Dibya had disappeared.

Clare and I had always been horror fans, particularly of zombie flicks and TV shows, so to her credit, my wife had believed me when I'd told her about Samir's message. OK, well, that wasn't exactly true. It was one thing to have a fondness for tall zombie tales; it was another thing entirely to trust such post-apocalyptic scenarios could really happen.

In all fairness, I'd had to play Samir's actual recording for her – a few times, in fact – before she'd accepted the new normal. Granted, Clare hadn't *wanted* to believe our friend's heartfelt warning, but she'd ultimately agreed to vacate our life in New Orleans before the three-week deadline.

Still, my wife would've hated seeing the courtyard in its present condition. Blood splatter covered the front of our grill. Our patio chairs lay in disarray, and whatever nasty goo had oozed out of both zombie heads now pooled around the legs of the plastic table holding our ultra-inexpensive washer and dryer.

With my head throbbing and my stomach grumbling for sustenance, I righted the chairs and rolled the undead pirate closer to the grill, away from the rear steps.

Big mistake.

The foul-smelling goop slowly spilling out of his head splashed all over the pavement.

It didn't really matter, of course. I'd never expected to return to the apartment once we were safely somewhere else. Clare wouldn't ever see the courtyard in such a nasty state. In fact, she'd never again encounter any of what had become, over the past four years of living there, our pride and joy.

Nabbing the apartment had marked the first time we'd ever had a private courtyard – quite a coup for renters in the French Quarter. Most courtyards in New Orleans, especially those in the city's oldest neighborhood, were either enjoyed by a single homeowner or, in the case of buildings turned into apartment complexes, shared by all the current tenants.

Our building, however, only housed three apartments: two in the front, along St. Ann Street, and ours in the rear, accessible via a gated side alley. Since we (and the landlord, if she were still alive) had the only keys to the gate, Clare and I had the courtyard all to ourselves. Not the roomiest space, but we'd still managed to transform it, within our small budget, into a cozy retreat, a place to grill our meals, host intimate crawfish boils, and relax with cocktails beside the fire pit – a sanctuary from the craziness of the Quarter.

Sadly, though, not one item from the courtyard had been part of my prep work for the oncoming zombie apocalypse, so it would all stay put.

My gaze shifted to the tiled table beside the grill, a faded red canvas umbrella sheltering it and the four encircling chairs from the sunlight. Clare and I had shared so many romantic meals at that table, so many card games and cocktails with friends. All that was over, though. Most of those friends were surely dead by now – either unwilling to believe Samir's warning or ill-prepared for the premature zombie onslaught.

To be honest, though, I'd never really liked most of them all that much. Besides, I had other shit to worry about. Like my family.

Tell me, at a time like this, is that wrong?

As I stared at the table, willing myself to go back inside, I heard soft grunts and shuffling footsteps coming from Tommy's courtyard. That decrepit wooden barrier – with its broken slats, rusted nails, and half-ass patches – was the only downside of our private oasis. For years, our landlord and the owners of the house behind us (that is, Tommy and his wife) had battled over who should repair the run-down fence, which just got weaker with every windstorm, rainfall, and hurricane. But at least my neighbor's ladder no longer pushed against the rotten wood, weakening it even more. I took momentary solace in that.

Momentary.

Of course, what happened next shouldn't have surprised me. I might've secured the front gate, but I'd done nothing to fortify the back fence. So, it did little to prevent two zombies from crashing through the already compromised slats, the sound of splintering wood jolting me from my reverie. The shuffling I'd heard had no doubt become a desperate sprint once the two creatures had caught a whiff of my scent.

"Son of a bitch!" I cursed as the first zombie slammed into me.

We both tumbled to the ground, where I once again smacked my head against the concrete steps.

This shit is getting old... real fast.

Chapter

3

"My easygoing nature is getting' sorely fuckin' tested."
– Bill Pardy, *Slither* (2006)

Fortunately, I didn't lose consciousness, but the pain still jostled my concentration. I had to stay focused and subdue the zombie quickly – not just to avoid being his breakfast, but also to liberate myself before the second zombie became a problem. The only thing preventing *him* from attacking me was that he'd inadvertently caught his coat on a nail jutting out from one of the fence supports. Given the crappy condition of the fence – and the zombie's apparent determination to reach me – I knew it wouldn't hold him for long.

I shifted my attention back to the creature on top of me. Based on the expensive suit he wore – presently spattered with blood, thanks to the gaping, ragged hole in his shoulder – he appeared to be a businessman of some kind. Maybe a lawyer or a banker or some other white-collar type that rarely endured a zombie apocalypse. At least in the movies.

Although the gore on his face made it hard to tell, the guy seemed to be about my age: mid-forties. But, damn, he must've worked out a bit more than I ever had. Even as a mindless zombie, the dude had unnatural strength.

As soon as the businessman had fallen on top of me, he'd grabbed my shirt and pulled himself toward my face. His weight threatened to suffocate me, and his gnashing teeth moved closer to my cheek. Luckily, the axe once again came in handy. It really was a solid zombie-killing device.

With some effort, I managed to push against the zombie's chest and simultaneously shove the axe handle into his mouth, smashing several of his once-perfect teeth in the process. Not that the dental dilemma stopped him. He simply responded by chewing on the wood with his remaining incisors, trying his damnedest to reach my hand. Putrid saliva, pus, and blood dripped onto my face as I slid the handle through his mouth. When the axe blade caught against his cheek, I yanked the handle downward and, amid horrendous cracking and snapping sounds, sliced his lower jaw away from his head.

More foulness gushed onto my skin and clothes, but luckily, I'd clamped my own jaws shut to avoid contamination. Besides, the distraction enabled me to wriggle out from beneath the businessman and roll him onto his back.

Stumbling to my feet, I glanced toward the other zombie, the one dressed like a familiar-looking cowboy – complete with tan pants, a maroon work shirt, a brown knee-length duster coat, a hip holster on his belt, and brown leather gloves, boots, and suspenders. I could only assume that he and the businessman had become compatriots after the zombie apocalypse began – and not before. Regardless, the cowboy still struggled against the same stubborn nail, the suede coat apparently too sturdy to tear easily.

Before I could deal with the hapless cowboy, the jawless businessman started to rise. With little hesitation, I set the axe on the table, picked up the spare propane tank beside the grill, heaved it above my head, and smashed it down onto his mangled face.

Four blows later, he lay motionless in a heap of gore, and my arms ached from the weight of the propane tank. Setting it on the ground, I kept my eyes on the bloody zombie, just in case he wasn't quite dead yet... although, the vile, shattered mess that used to be his head should've been my first clue he wasn't coming back. The chunks of skull and putrid brain matter dripping from the propane tank only solidified that fact.

A ripping sound alerted me to his partner's presence. The cowboy had finally broken free of the fence and stumbled through the foliage lining the courtyard. Hastily, I inverted one of our patio chairs, snagged him with the legs before he could reach me, and maneuvered him to the right side of the building.

Three large air-conditioning units (one for each apartment), plus ladders, hoses, and various tools, filled the narrow alley, rendering it more of a cramped storage area than a pathway to St. Ann Street (unlike the alley on the other side). In addition, thick brown vines covered the ground, snaking around the A/C units and making it easy to trip. I'd once watched a repairman take a nasty tumble there, so I figured I could simply prod the cowboy – actually, he looked more like a certain *space* cowboy – with the chair and push him over the first A/C unit.

Although I managed to pin him against the metal frame, my victory didn't last long. With the surprising strength and stamina of a fresh zombie (at least according to Hollywood), he pushed the chair aside and immediately righted himself. Luckily, before he could get close to me, he slipped on a vine and smacked his temple on a corner of the A/C.

I hoped the blow to his head had killed him, but after a moment, he again rose to his feet.

What the fuck?

Seriously, the left side of the guy's face had caved inward, but his brain was somehow still active, and he clearly hadn't given up his desire to eat me.

While moving forward, he accidentally stepped inside a nest of vines. Both of his boots snagged the root-like foliage, and he fell forward onto the pavement, his lower half trapped as if in quicksand. He tried to wriggle out of the vines, but the more he fidgeted, the more tangled he became.

The space cowboy had finally grounded himself. Of

course, I kicked his head anyway – just for good measure.

Chapter

4

"It's Halloween. Everyone's entitled to one good scare." – Brackett, *Halloween* (1978)

Leaving the space cowboy to his own tangled mess, I returned the chair to its rightful spot and retrieved the axe from the table. With a towel I'd accidentally left in our covered dryer, I did my best to wipe off my face as well as the axe. The bloody feathers, fur, and hide had seen better days, but at least the blade was relatively clean. An effective zombie killer, it would make a solid addition to the lengthy list of weapons I'd purchased while preparing for the apocalypse.

In our more than seventeen years together, Clare and I had never had a lot of money. Figuring what little we did possess would be pretty useless once the zombie chaos started, I'd decided I might as well spend it all preparing for the end.

So, after having persuaded Clare to trust Samir's insane message, I'd started buying everything I thought we'd need for our hasty exodus from the city. I'd even chronicled the entire process on my blog, which, by the end, had only attracted about a hundred readers.

Not bad for such a short run, though I doubted it had done any good. Even those who'd "believed" me were probably not prepared for how batshit-crazy the situation would get.

For the benefit of my meager audience, I'd cataloged everything I'd bought and why. Kept urging people to prepare for doomsday, striving to convince them of the government's lies, hoping to make them believe the infected dead would really, truly rise. I'd blogged every night, for the first nine days of my preparations, then my blog had experienced "technical difficulties" and no longer appeared.

Fucking government.

Guess I should be grateful Clare and I hadn't disappeared along with my public ramblings.

Anyway... the people who'd followed my blog generally fell into one of two categories. First, those entertained by the rantings of a lunatic, chiding me with their inane comments, claiming I was just another unhinged nut seeking attention for his crazy conspiracy theories. But, right or wrong, they kept giving me the attention I supposedly craved.

The rest of my readers considered themselves doomsday preppers. While most of them weren't the sort of folks I'd want to socialize with on a regular basis, they certainly shared a lot of decent ideas and ultimately steered me in the right direction for some of my survival prep work.

Following the curious shutdown of my blog, I'd simply continued to gather supplies and ready us for life during the zombie chaos, periodically combing the web for any mention of what was happening in America and overseas. Not surprisingly, there hadn't been much in the way of accurate news.

Then, fourteen days into the twenty-one-day countdown – and yes, we'd intended to leave town before the very end – Clare had decided to head to Baton Rouge. The reason? She'd hoped to convince her mom to come with us when we fled north.

Now, just to be clear, Clare's mother had despised me ever since we'd gotten married fifteen years earlier, so the idea of her coming with us didn't exactly thrill me. Then again, compared to the imminent apocalypse, she was the least of my worries. And Jill's presence was bound to put Clare at ease, which might even make the whole trip less stressful for me.

In essence, our plan was to head north to my parents' property in northern Michigan and hopefully ride out the storm (so to speak). Clare, who admittedly hated driving, had reluctantly ventured the eighty miles to Baton Rouge by herself, while I'd stayed behind to finish loading up the old step van I'd purchased.

After much tug-of-war between me (the purger) and my wife (the hoarder), I'd managed to pack up or ship out almost everything of importance (including a small, nonnegotiable selection of Clare's photos, jewelry, and other memorabilia). Following my final supply trip to the secure lot where we kept our van, the only precious items left included a go-bag and our furry child: Azazel, a seven-year-old, short-haired tabby.

We'd named her after a demon because she hated

everyone except me and Clare. Her fickle personality had always bothered my wife, but I, on the other hand, thought it was hilarious. She was my attack cat, meant to keep people away, and I had to admit, I'd always loved watching Clare's mother try to pet her every time she visited and, without fail, receive a hiss (and, once, a bite) for her trouble.

It's the little things that make life worth living.

The fourteenth day of my pre-zombie grace period had fallen on Halloween, normally a big deal for everyone in the Big Easy. Like children everywhere else in America, the kids down there dressed up and went trick-or-treating door to door, but the adults were another story. New Orleanians would embrace any opportunity for a party, and Halloween was no different. It was also one of the rare occasions Clare and I relished meandering through the French Quarter – mainly to check out the creative costumes and joyous mayhem.

Didn't hurt that women typically took the chance to don the sluttiest outfits imaginable. Whether they'd decided to dress as a vampire, a cop, a superhero, a nurse, or something else altogether, they would almost always choose the most scantily clad version.

During one Halloween a few years earlier, Clare and I

had been in a strip club (where the women typically fawned over her) when in walked a priest and a nun.

Sounds like the beginning of a bad joke, but it's true.

At first, we'd thought it was just a pair of religious nut jobs – the ones who often tried to convert tourists doing the "Bourbon crawl" (that is, strolling from bar to bar, getting blotto on Bourbon Street, as only college students, conventioneers, and first-time visitors to New Orleans could do). Expecting a lecture from the overzealous Christians, we'd been pleasantly surprised when they sat at a table and ordered high-priced cocktails instead.

Almost immediately, the nun had bought herself a lap dance, and the lucky lady she'd chosen was soon sliding her hands up the nun's tunic, past her stockings, all the way to the Promised Land. Safe to say everyone in the club, including me and Clare, had opted to watch the girl-on-girl lap dance instead of the solo dancers on stage.

Yeah, we loved New Orleans at Halloween – and sadly, we'd missed the latest one. But, given the ever-increasing pile of zombified bodies lying in my courtyard, that didn't seem like such a bad thing.

While Bourbon Street was packed on most nights,

Halloween could become as dangerously crowded as Mardi Gras. Wall-to-wall people shoving their way up and down the street. Not the best place to be during a zombie epidemic.

Still, since we'd thought we had more time, that wasn't exactly the reason we'd ignored our favorite holiday. Frankly, with Armageddon on the horizon, neither of us had felt all that festive. So, instead of venturing out for one last drunken, costumed spectacle, Clare had decided to skip the festivities altogether, borrow a friend's car, and head for her mom's place with the misguided plan of persuading her to join us on our mad dash up north.

I, meanwhile, had opted to stay at home on All Hallows' Eve, not only to finish packing, but also because the Quarter mayhem was never as much fun without my partner in crime. I just hoped, given what had happened in the Big Easy, Clare was safe at my mother-in-law's house. Surveying the bloody, body-filled area that had once served as our private sanctuary, I decided the time had come to get out of town, head to Michigan's Lower Peninsula, and snatch my wife along the way.

Chapter

5

"I can't profess to understand God's plan. Christ promised the resurrection of the dead. I just thought he had something a little different in mind." – Hershel Greene, *The Walking Dead* (2012)

Before grabbing the last of my stuff, I crept toward the gate and listened for any activity in the street. One aspect of the courtyard Clare and I had always enjoyed was the bizarre way it dulled sound. We could often hear our neighbors along the sides and at the rear – particularly when they had rowdy company – but street sounds were faint at best.

Honking car horns, rumbling delivery trucks, and blaring karaoke songs from the gay bar on the opposite corner were all much less obnoxious than they might've seemed from the two front apartments. The clip-clopping mules, creaking carriage wheels, and cackling late-night revelers headed toward Bourbon Street were less intrusive, too.

The courtyard walls, plus the houses surrounding us, provided a barrier of insulation between our hidden oasis and the outside world. Oftentimes, Clare and I would find it difficult to know what was happening on St. Ann without venturing to the gate for a look-see. Even Mardi Gras parades – including our favorite, the dog-centric Krewe of Barkus – had passed by the building without disturbing the relative peace and quiet of our courtyard.

The night before, however, had been an unusual situation. I'd been preparing a quick dinner in the kitchen when I heard the first screams. Right away, I'd realized those weren't the normal sounds of drunken revelry but, rather, bloodcurdling shrieks of a much more fucked-up nature.

After snatching the decorative axe from the wall, I'd slipped out the door, tiptoed down the alley, and opened the gate, only to be rewarded with my first encounter with a zombie. The very same undead pirate lying in my courtyard, oozing foulness from his head.

As I currently approached the gate, I didn't discern much of anything – just a few shouts, groans, and gunshots in the distance. Similar to the sounds I'd often perceived in the French Quarter. In a way, it was worse than hearing the screams of living victims, since it implied most of the people in the Quarter had been either killed or turned during the late-night and early-morning hours.

Then, as I strained my ears, I gradually heard it. A perpetual buzzing sound, like the droning made by a hive of hungry bees in a rose garden.

Slowly, I unlocked the gate, tightened my grip on the axe, and stepped onto the sidewalk, hoping my curiosity wouldn't result in the same antics I'd experienced the night before.

Immediately, I noticed dead bodies in the road. A lot of bodies, in fact. Partially eaten, lying in haphazard piles, their costumes torn and bloody. Even worse than the mangled corpses, though, were the body parts: just random heads, limbs, and torsos, like what you'd see in the aftermath of a terrible plane crash... or the lair of a rogue alligator. If the street cleaners who scoured the Quarter biweekly were still in business, they had quite a task ahead of them.

A tuft of bloody fur caught my eye, and stepping closer, I realized humans weren't the only victims splayed along St. Ann. Amid the costumes and gore lay several feral cats and leashed dogs, too. Obviously, no living organism was immune to a zombie's hunger.

I felt more sadness for the lost animals than the deceased people. Not a revelation for me: I'd always preferred cats, dogs, goats, elephants, and other innocent creatures to my fellow humans. People usually hated me for those beliefs.

And I just hate them right back.

The buzzing had increased as I'd neared the asphalt roadway, and I could finally see the reason why. Hundreds of flies hovered, dove, and landed on the corpses, doing what flies did best: scavenging from the dead. Numerous rats crawled and nibbled their way across the bodies, too. I wondered if sampling from the zombies' victims would turn them into undead insects and rodents. If so, I hoped they couldn't spread the infection to other unsuspecting animals and humans. As if it weren't already a plague to end all plagues.

Familiar scents wafted in the autumn breeze: stale hints of urine, vomit, feces, beer, and trash, just as typical in the French Quarter as the more pleasant aromas of coffee, boiled seafood, and sweet olive trees. But, beyond such common odors, I noted a burning smell on the wind, like that of a distant fire.

Worse, though, was the oppressive stench emanating from the bodies, so foul it was actually making me dizzy. I'd never known much about how fast a body could decay, but it seemed as if the corpses were more rancid than I'd expected. Maybe that was due to the mangled body parts, covered with every kind of gore you'd never want to imagine.

Glancing up and down the street, I didn't see anything – or anyone – in motion. No breathing, no twitching, no struggling to stand. Despite the horrifying scene, I found the relative stillness reassuring: At least those victims were too brain-dead to be reanimated.

Then, I noted movement in my peripheral vision. Turning my head to the right, I spotted a young woman dragging herself down Burgundy Street. From a distance, I couldn't see the details of her face, but she appeared to be missing the lower half of her left leg. She was either one tough survivor – or a zombie on a mission.

When she paused to taste a fallen police officer, I had my answer. After a bite or two, she crawled over the uniformed torso.

Guess the body isn't fresh enough for her.

"What're you doing out here, Joe?"

The unexpected sound almost flatlined my heart rate. It took a few seconds to recognize the voice of the crotchety old man who lived in one of the front apartments of my building. He was standing above me, his slippered feet planted on the small stoop to my right. I'd been too distracted by the carnage to notice him.

"For fuck's sake, Robert," I said, glancing upward. "I almost pissed myself."

Chuckling, he eyed my gore-stained face, clothes, and hands. "Good to see you made it. Since I didn't hear any noise in your apartment, I thought you might've bitten the dust."

Clare and I had warned as many friends, relatives, and neighbors about the impending zombie apocalypse as we could. Unfortunately, most of them, having thought we'd finally seen one too many horror flicks, had simply stopped speaking to us.

Though Robert wasn't one of the naysayers, he'd never seemed convinced by Samir's news. Even after we'd played him the audio file. But his calm demeanor in the wake of the Big Easy bloodbath made me suspect he'd either believed us all along or, despite his usual unwillingness to change, adapted to the new normal quickly.

"Nope, still here." I glanced toward the partially open door behind him, where a scuffed, disturbingly bloody baseball bat leaned against the jamb. "Where's Carolina?"

Carolina was Robert's only obvious companion, an aging greyhound who would more often whimper and trot for cover than bark and stand her ground in the face of danger. Loud trucks, thunderstorms, and fireworks terrified her most of all.

He sighed. "Where else? Cowering under the bed upstairs. Ever since the screaming started, she's refused to come out."

"Can't say I blame her. I'm sure Azazel's not too happy either." And I wasn't too pleased to realize Azazel and Carolina would be just as tempting to a zombie as I had been. Blinking away the image of dead pets in the street, I shifted my focus toward the other front stoop, a few yards to the right of Robert. "Have you seen Allison?"

Allison was our other neighbor, a bitter, thirtysomething Goth chick who'd rarely told me and Clare "hello," much less stopped to chat with us.

He shook his head. "She and her boyfriend went away for Halloween. Wanted to spend the night in the doll room at Myrtles." He chuckled again. "The Quarter always did attract freaks and weirdos."

As usual, I refrained from contradicting Robert. No point in admitting Clare and I, self-confessed horror nuts, had long dreamed of staying in the infamously creepy, doll-filled bedroom at the Myrtles Plantation, the supposedly haunted mansion in St. Francisville.

Robert nodded toward the woman slithering across the bodies on Burgundy, and I followed his gaze.

"I know that little bitch," he said sardonically. "She tended bar over at Lafitte's. Cut me off once. Serves her right."

I stared at my neighbor of four years. "Really? For that, she deserves to be a zombie?"

He shrugged, as unapologetic as always.

If Robert had lived in a suburban house, with a yard of

his own, instead of a French Quarter apartment, he probably would've been the quintessential curmudgeon on the block, the sort of old man who'd frequently yell, "Hey, you fucking hoodlums, get off my lawn!" at the top of his alcohol-soaked lungs.

At least, most people in the neighborhood viewed him that way.

Clare and I actually liked the guy. Over the years, we'd often brought him containers of homemade gumbo and jambalaya, let him wash his clothes in our washer and dryer, and visited with him and Carolina on the way home from collecting our mail, dropping off our rent payment, or running to one of the nearby grocery stores.

In exchange for such limited companionship, Robert regularly checked on our place during the summer months, when we'd typically head to northern Michigan to escape the oppressive heat of southern Louisiana.

Still, Robert had a reputation as one of the most disagreeable neighbors in the Quarter. He'd routinely report homeowners for violating the rules of the Vieux Carré Commission, shout at motorists who littered or played their music too loud, and holler at bicyclists who went the wrong direction on one-way St. Ann or sailed past the stop sign at the Dauphine intersection.

Once, I'd even witnessed him picking up a pile of shit some thoughtless dog owner had failed to bag. Then, before I could question him, he'd impressed me by throwing it twenty yards, pegging said owner in the head. That made Robert more than OK in my book.

Naturally, the fact that I understood and condoned Robert's behavior disturbed my wife, who worried I would become an even grouchier old man someday. But, what could I say? Robert amused me – and made a lot of sense to boot. I found most humans to be just as selfish and inconsiderate as he did. Probably didn't help my case that he seemed to prefer us to the rest of the neighbors, too.

Unfortunately, the female zombie Robert and I had observed was eyeballing us with a ravenous expression. Whether she'd heard our voices or smelled our flesh hadn't made a difference. Obviously, the decaying organs in the road weren't nearly as tantalizing as the fresh meat standing in front of our building.

"Shit." He grabbed the baseball bat and held it against his right shoulder. "I think she's coming over here."

Fucking fantastic. Just what I need. Another hungry zombie to fend off.

"Listen, Robert, I'm getting outta town. Clare's already at her mother's place in Baton Rouge." I glanced toward the crawling girl, who was making decent progress over the bodies strewn across St. Ann. "I think you should come with me."

"Nah, I've lived in this neighborhood for over forty years." He gripped his bat with both hands, readying himself for a fight. "Goddamn zombies aren't gonna chase me off."

I shook my head, realizing that would likely be the last time I ever saw Robert alive. Sadly, I'd already experienced too many last times – and no doubt, there would be plenty more.

I backed toward the open gateway behind me. "Alright, man. If you're sure..."

"I'm sure." He looked down at me and winked. "But thanks."

"OK, then, good luck."

"Same to you and Clare."

Leaving my neighbor to deal with the stingy zombified bartender, I once again retreated behind my gate. It was well past time to go. I just needed to grab what remained of the stuff we planned to take with us, prod Azazel into her carrier, and try to reach our vehicle with as little violence and mayhem as possible.

Shit.

I paused halfway down the alley, beside Robert's kitchen window. I'd almost forgotten: There was still one stop I had to make before leaving town, and it was nonnegotiable.

Chapter

6

"I'm your number one fan. There's nothing to worry about. You're going to be just fine. I will take good care of you. I'm your number one fan." – Annie Wilkes, *Misery* (1990)

Sighing in aggravation, I continued toward the courtyard. As I emerged into the disheveled, gore-covered space, I surveyed the three smashed zombies, the large gaping hole in our broken fence, and the fidgeting creature still trapped by the vines. The pirate, the cook, and the businessman were no longer a problem, but I didn't want the space cowboy – or the busted fence – to become a dilemma for Robert.

Since he'd decided to remain in New Orleans, he would have enough of a challenge staying alive without being attacked by surprise from the rear of the building. If too many zombies wandered into the courtyard and crowded toward the front gate, some of the more determined creatures might climb atop one another and reach the side windows that led into his living room and kitchen. For all I knew about zombies, some of them might even try to slither beneath the raised house and claw their way through the floorboards.

True, it was Robert's dumbass choice to stay in Zombietown. I'd offered him a chance to leave, and I couldn't do much more to protect him from himself – or any of the undead left in the Quarter. But even with my less-than-stellar conscience, I couldn't leave him so vulnerable either.

Gazing at the facedown cowboy, I tried to figure out

how to neutralize him without getting into chomping range. I could've used my trusty axe, but I didn't want to risk tripping amid the vines and receive a fatal bite for my trouble.

As an alternative, I placed the axe atop the covered dryer and dragged an old two-by-four from beneath the building. Leftover lumber from the previous Halloween, when I'd built an outdoor movie screen in the courtyard and treated me, Clare, and some of our closest friends to a horror flick marathon.

Slowly, I approached the space cowboy. When he finally noticed me, his wriggling became more frenetic. He extended his arms forward and swung them in a frenzied, crisscrossed pattern, obviously trying to grab me.

Given that the two-by-four was nearly six feet long, I could thankfully avoid getting too close to his outstretched hands. Standing just shy of his leather gloves, I slammed the plank onto his head. A pained moan rumbled from his throat, and black ooze squirted from his nose, making me gag a little before I hit him again.

Not surprisingly, the Captain Mal lookalike had a hard head. It required seven skull-crushing swings before he finally stopped twitching. Surely, any remaining *Firefly* fans would forgive the insult, but regardless, that space cowboy needed to be put down.

Once he was no longer a threat, I set down the bloody, brain-flecked two-by-four and glanced at the gaping hole in the fence. Luckily, the thumping and groaning noises hadn't lured any more zombies into the adjacent courtyard. Afraid to press my luck, I didn't linger for long.

Instead, I stepped over the cowboy and picked up the old box-spring leaning against my side neighbor's wall. With a sheet pulled tautly across it, the box-spring had served as a decent movie screen for the previous year's Halloween party. After countless rainstorms had rendered it soggy, rusted, and useless as a screen, it would finally have a newfound purpose as a zombie barrier. Suddenly, I was grateful I hadn't heeded Clare's repeated requests to toss it in a nearby dumpster.

I lifted the box-spring over the dead cowboy and set it against the gap in the ragged fence. With some effort, I hefted my heavy grill over the dead pirate and onto the flower box to pin the box-spring in place. Then, I slid the patio table and our giant heating lamp against the grill for some added fortification. Hopefully, the barrier would hold. At least for a little while.

Of course, like the incompetent Army Corps of Engineers who'd merely patched the levee breaches following Hurricane Katrina – only to weaken the rest of the structure – I'd just succeeded in securing the hole, nothing more. The rest of the fence was still woefully inadequate as protection. Wouldn't take much for a hungry zombie to bust through the weaker slats. I could only hope the large, thorny bougainvillea bush beside the pile of junk would deter any flesh-seeking creatures – or at least slow them down a bit.

Chapter

7

"You have created a monster, and it will destroy you."
– Dr. Waldman, *Frankenstein* (1931)

Convinced I'd done all I could in the courtyard, I picked up the axe, bypassed the oozing zombie bodies on the ground, and trudged up the steps. As I entered the cramped foyer, a crushing wave of sadness hit me. Clare and I had made the simple, one-bedroom apartment our home. For the past four years, we'd spent a lot of time renovating it to take full advantage of every square inch – from building extra storage shelves in the bedroom and bathroom to adding a cat-sized viewing platform next to the lowest glass pane in our door.

True, we'd never sought our landlord's permission for such alterations – a fact that rankled my rule-abiding wife. But, according to the landlord's head maintenance man, no tenant had ever received approval for a construction project. Whenever we decided to give up the apartment, we could only hope the wacky, temperamental lawyer who owned our building (and many structures throughout the Quarter) would appreciate the redesign and merely keep our security deposit in lieu of suing us.

Now that Armageddon had come, though, it didn't really matter anymore, and after all our hard work, we had to abandon the place anyway. In the end, we still lost our deposit – not due to a disgruntled landlord, but because of a fucking zombie apocalypse. Who could've predicted such a thing? And how, frankly, would more money have helped us anyway?

Money, like so many assets and commodities of an eradicated civilization, no longer meant what it had. Guns, bullets, fuel, water, food, alcohol, medicine, and toilet paper would be the primary currencies in the new undead world.

Yep, that's right. Fucking toilet paper.

You might laugh, but bath tissue would now be as good as gold. How many people wanted to wipe their asses with their hands? Not many, I'd bet.

One of the preppers who'd followed my blog had filled his entire attic with toilet paper and booze. He would fare well in the new bartering economy.

Standing in the foyer, with my wife over eighty miles away, I still found it hard to accept the truth: The cozy apartment, where Clare and I had made and shared so many wonderful memories, would no longer be our home.

Glancing to my right, I smiled wistfully at my favorite enhancement. I'd sliced a large hole in the wall between the small foyer and the even tinier kitchen, installed shelves and a countertop, and painted everything a cool mint green, creating a pleasant breakfast nook. As a bonus, I'd also improved the kitchen space, bringing in natural light from the large window and partial glass door in the foyer and providing the counter space I required for cooking.

In our old life, our roles had been simple: I was the cook, Clare was the dishwasher. Jobs that had pleased us both – although I'd sometimes doubted her claim she found washing dishes meditative. Tidying up my messes couldn't have been easy, but she'd rarely complained. She'd just seemed grateful I enjoyed cooking so much – which I always had, since before I'd even gone to college.

As a native Midwesterner, I'd especially embraced the cuisine of New Orleans, my wife's hometown. The zombie apocalypse depressed me for lots of reasons, not the least of which was knowing my limited stores of cayenne pepper, filé powder, and other local ingredients wouldn't last forever. How would I survive in the future without regular doses of seafood gumbo, jambalaya, and shrimp Creole?

Red beans and rice would be less problematic, but once the ham and sausage supplies had vanished, the traditional "laundry day" dish wouldn't be nearly as digestible. At least for me. Clare, as I'd learned at the beginning of our relationship, would pretty much eat anything – even moldy fruit and other foods well past their expiration date. Often to her detriment.

The only minor advantage of the apocalypse – besides the chance to thin out the assholes and reboot civilization – was that I no longer had to remove my shoes each time I entered our apartment. Since our decision to leave town, Clare had lifted the no-shoes policy that kept us from tracking all manner of French Quarter filth, from urine to vomit, into the house. With three weeks left before the end (or so we'd thought), we just hadn't had time to waste on our germaphobic tendencies.

Gazing at my blood-speckled sneakers, though, I couldn't help but laugh. A few weeks earlier, zombie goo would've been the last thing we'd have feared bringing into our home.

I stepped into the small living room, which, thanks to the traditionally high ceilings of the French Quarter, we'd been able to turn into our own private movie theater. I'd installed a high-end projector, a surround-sound system, and an eight-foot-tall electronic screen, which we could raise and lower with the touch of a button.

Our home theater setup had offered hours of late-night pleasure for me and my fellow film buff, but while the screen would remain there in perpetuity, the projector was long gone. I'd shipped it north during my preparations for abandoning the city. What better time, after all, to escape into the movies than during a zombie apocalypse?

As I stood in the living room, clutching the axe and surveying our framed sci-fi and horror show posters one last time, I heard a plaintive meow emerge from the adjacent room. My eyes shifted to the wine-red curtain that separated the living room from our small bedroom.

A few seconds later, Azazel slunk beneath the curtain

and squinted at me with the *give-me-a-treat-now!* expression she usually reserved for Clare. She'd been alone all night, ever since I'd left my half-prepared dinner on the counter and ended up knocked out in the courtyard. Not surprisingly, she was seeking some attention – whether treats or a chin scratch would satisfy her, it likely didn't make a difference.

Spotting the sticky gore on my knuckles, I opted not to infect my cat with zombie germs. Instead, I took a moment to wash my hands in the kitchen sink before reaching down and scratching the soft white fur under her chin.

"Sorry, girl. I got delayed a bit. But now, we need to go get your mama."

Meowing pleadingly, she gazed toward the top of the fridge, where we normally kept her kibble and treats (most of which, along with an extra litter box and some of her favorite toys, were already in the van). Instinctively, I glanced at her food and water bowls, both of which were now empty. She must've cleaned them out while I lay bleeding in the courtyard.

"I know you're hungry. I am, too. But we have to get outta here."

Besides, Clare and I never give you food or water

before a big road trip.

Though a pretty laidback traveler (for a cat), Azazel had a tendency to get an upset stomach while in motion. No need to fuel the fire – and end up with yet another mess on top of everything else.

Still, I could sympathize with her. In addition to filling my rumbling stomach, I wouldn't have minded treating my head wound either. Unfortunately, I had precious little time to waste.

To her credit, Azazel seemed to understand the urgency of the situation. Without her usual fuss, she allowed me to scoop her up and guide her into the carrier. Once I'd latched the gate, she settled down on her blanket and waited for my next move.

After pausing to wonder if I'd forgotten to pack anything essential, I tossed the previous night's half-made dinner into an open, half-filled garbage bag and wolfed down two granola bars for a much-needed energy spike. Then, I popped two aspirin for my brain-splitting headache (no doubt amplified by my extreme hunger and lack of caffeine) and drained half a bottle of diet soda.

Lastly, I picked up Azazel's bowls and tucked them inside my "go-bag" – the supply-laden satchel preppers usually grabbed when they had to leave somewhere in a hurry. Just a glorified backpack, my go-bag still lay unzipped on the bed, waiting for any last-minute weapons, tools, food, or other supplies.

I spotted my cellphone beside the bag and picked it up, hoping for a message from Clare. But even though I'd been unconscious all night, no voicemail or text messages awaited me. I was worried; it would've eased my mind to hear her voice. So, I tried calling her, but not surprisingly, the circuits were jammed. For the foreseeable future, nobody would be able to reach anyone.

Gazing at the open satchel, I felt so stupid for having painted myself into a corner. I might've had my go-bag, but I'd stowed all the guns, crossbows, blades, and other weapons in the van. I hadn't wanted to carry them out in the open, afraid that, if a cop stopped me, he'd arrest me for my illegal arsenal, so I'd packed them earlier in the process and failed to leave myself anything to fight with. The zombie-killing axe would have to do.

While considering the stained weapon, I noticed the gore on my T-shirt and jeans. Although I was eager to reunite with Clare, I didn't think my wife would appreciate seeing me covered in zombie brains and blood. So, I stripped off my clothes and shoes, jumped in the shower, and wiped the guck off my face and hair. Then, after donning some fresh apparel and disinfecting the gash on my skull, I checked each room for any other necessities.

Satisfied I had everything I needed, I zipped up the go-bag, swung it over my shoulder, and slipped my wallet and the van keys in my back pockets. I dumped my soiled clothes and sneakers in the last garbage bag and secured it with a twist-tie. Though unwilling to let the trash rot in our former home, I fully realized no city worker would ever claim it from the can in the courtyard.

Guess it's true what they say... old habits die hard.

I tucked the axe behind my belt and picked up Azazel's carrier. Then, taking one more look around – at the apartment I'd never see again, at the stove where I'd prepared so many yummy pots of gumbo, at the couch where Clare and I had watched so many movies on our huge-ass screen – the sadness suddenly left me. Anger quickly replaced it.

"Fucking assholes, you screwed the whole world," I muttered to myself, loud enough to wake up Azazel, her wide green eyes watching me warily through the slits of her carrier.

Right then, the lights in the kitchen went off, the ceiling fan above me slowed down, and the refrigerator's hum fell silent. The apartment was eerily quiet, with meager streams of daylight coming through the frosted kitchen window and the glass panes in the foyer door.

"Just fucking perfect. Couldn't wait another hour before going off?"

If the power had gone out in the entire Quarter, that would make my exodus from the city even tougher. Our van sat in a parking lot behind two giant swinging doors – controlled by the electric garage-door opener in my backpack.

Oh, well. Time to go.

I'd deal with that minor dilemma once I got there. Just needed to make one quick stop first – and pray I wouldn't run into any complications along the way.

Chapter

8

"This is no dream! This is really happening!" – Rosemary Woodhouse, *Rosemary's Baby* (1968)

After pointlessly dumping my trash in the outdoor garbage can and momentarily lingering in our former-sanctuary-turned-zombie-graveyard, I headed up the alley one last time. At the front gate, I protectively held Azazel's carrier behind me, leaned against the wood, and listened for any sounds coming from the street. Besides the persistent buzzing of the flies, I could make out a strange thwacking sound, like someone repeatedly hitting a wet punching bag.

Slowly, I opened the gate. Just a crack. Just in case.

When no undead face greeted my own, I swung open the gate and stepped onto the sidewalk. Immediately, I spotted Robert, standing on his front stoop, hunched over the zombie bartender, who had apparently slithered up the steps and almost reached his door.

Granted, she was no longer in a condition to slither anywhere. Her head now resembled the consistency, if not the vibrant color, of a smashed overripe watermelon, and yet, Robert continued to beat her brain pulp with his gore-covered baseball bat.

"That's for cutting me off!" he shouted, whacking her again.

OK, so I did get the chance to see my skinny old neighbor one more time. Honestly, though, I wished I hadn't.

Following the epic smackdown between the young woman's skull and Robert's trusty bat, he couldn't hide the evidence. Blood, brain bits, and black ooze clung to his hands, face, and worn terrycloth robe. Each downward swing onto the unfortunate girl's head resulted in a new spatter of zombie goo. And all for what? Some end-of-shift stinginess in a French Quarter bar?

OK, fine, maybe the zombified version of her deserved some comeuppance.

Somehow, though, I suspected his anger was misdirected. Like me, he had long been a grouch and a misanthrope, but also like me, he probably didn't think a zombie apocalypse would be the best solution for humanity's problems. Thumping the undead buzzkill on his front stoop was merely a substitute for taking down the powers-that-be who'd allowed the end-of-the-world crisis to happen. Still, for all we knew, those people – along with Samir and Dibya – were already dead.

Or deadish.

Gazing past my neighbor's stoop, I observed a large undead herd shambling along Burgundy. "Robert, you better go back inside. Those zombies might spot you."

Sure enough, two of the creatures swiveled their heads toward my old neighbor. Lured by either the whomping sounds or his tempting smell, they abruptly turned onto St. Ann and made a beeline for his front steps. Like mindless lemmings, the rest followed suit, but unlike the bludgeoned bartender, those zombies weren't crawling. In fact, they appeared to be trotting.

All at once, Robert stopped hitting the girl's motionless body. "Fuck."

I set Azazel's carrier on the ground, closed the gate, and made sure it was locked. More out of habit than from any real concern for the belongings I'd left behind – though, I had to admit, I hated the idea of looters or zombies trashing our house.

As Robert retreated from the dead bartender and stepped into his open doorway, he paused to gaze down at me. "Goin' to get Clare?"

I nodded, smiling at the thought of seeing my wife again. But my grin soon morphed into a frown. Abruptly, I'd realized that, while his harsh beating of the poor bartender had alerted the zombies to our presence, I was the one who would need to make a break for it.

"Good luck, boy," he said, slipping inside his apartment.

Well, shit.

I didn't have time to say goodbye – much less tell him about the blocked fence in the courtyard – before he slammed the front door and shoved something heavy against it, blocking the window that, as with my own door, inconveniently filled the upper half.

Without further hesitation, I picked up Azazel's carrier, pulled the axe from my belt, and darted to the corner. I turned toward the Lower Quarter and hastened down Dauphine Street, hurdling over dead, fly-peppered, rat-covered bodies wherever they lay. Given my poor conditioning and the awkward imbalance of toting a thirteen-pound cat over decomposing obstacles – with the carrier banging against my left thigh and the go-bag whacking my lower back – I wasn't shocked when I felt winded a half-block later.

Unfortunately, while pausing to catch my breath, I spotted several zombies stumbling down Dauphine, headed directly toward me. Still a couple blocks away, they were closing fast, and considering my next turn lay between me and them, I didn't have time to rest. Even if my lungs cried out for a break.

Although Samir and Dibya had given me fair warning about the imminent apocalypse and granted me enough time to amass a bunch of survival gear, I would've needed at least six months (if not more) to get into solid fighting and running shape. I wasn't in the worst condition for my age – maybe I'd put on twenty pounds since Clare and I had gotten married (OK, more like forty pounds) – but I typically walked three miles, twice a day, so I wasn't exactly inactive.

Still, the stitch in my side had already made me its bitch, and my heart threatened to pound itself out of my chest – not from exertion but from fear. I hadn't had time to get scared when the zombies attacked me (one at a time, I might add) in the courtyard, but staring at a slew of undead about to get a whiff of my tasty flesh, I panicked I wouldn't be able to withstand a gang attack.

Luckily, a woman's startling shriek diverted most of them onto St. Philip Street. Even with a few of them still headed my way, I decided I shouldn't bolt. Smarter to opt for a power walk or maybe a slow jog, but not a full-out run. As I moved toward Dumaine, the next cross street, the woman's screams abruptly ended.

Sorry, lady.

At that precise moment, I finally noticed the level of yelling and gunfire around me. Beside my gate, I'd heard the terrifying sounds in the distance, but the havoc was much closer than I'd realized. The odors of fire and rotting flesh had grown more pronounced – the fires were almost as disconcerting as the zombies. In a neighborhood like the

Quarter, where the buildings huddled close together – with few gaps, plenty of trees, and too many wooden fences – fire could spread like a wrathful god had soaked the neighborhood in gasoline.

Prior to the zombie apocalypse, the local fire department had taken blazes seriously in the Quarter; its response time had been way more prompt than that of incompetent NOPD officers to the scene of a mugging, rape, or murder. No one wanted a repeat of the Great New Orleans Fires of 1788 and 1794 that had destroyed most of the structures in the historic neighborhood, particularly since, by the twenty-first century, it had become ground zero for the city's tourism industry. But I doubted many firefighters were left to operate the hoses.

I couldn't believe I'd been so clueless – and not just about the encroaching fires. I'd been so focused on my own situation back at the house, the truth simply hadn't registered. Amid the decomposing corpses, a lot of people – living people – were still fighting for their lives against hungry zombies. In both directions on Dauphine and Dumaine, I witnessed life-or-death battles taking place in the streets and alleys, on the sidewalks and driveways, even on rickety galleries and balconies.

I needed to get the hell out of there and reach my wife

as soon as possible. So, striving to ignore the angry shouts, tearful pleas, breaking glass, and frenzied gunshots in all directions, I bypassed the zombies in my path and continued toward St. Philip.

Chapter

9

"Be afraid. Be very afraid." – Veronica Quaife, *The Fly* (1986)

Farther along Dauphine, a preppy guy clung to an old-fashioned gas lamppost. Given his bloodshot eyes and wobbly legs, he was obviously drunk. Never a shocking sight on All Saints' Day, but how the idiot had managed to stay alive was a complete mystery to me. The only weapon he carried was a bottle of tequila. Empty, of course.

Our eyes locked, and he smiled faintly, but from his squinting expression, I assumed he couldn't see me all that clearly. When my focus shifted past him, to the scantily clad, blood-splattered, zombified teenager shuffling toward him, he lazily followed my gaze to the approaching girl.

Unfortunately, he was either too bleary-eyed or too brain-numbed (or both) to recognize the danger, so when she was merely twenty feet from him, he slurred, "Hey, baby! Show me your tits!"

An only-in-New-Orleans kind of thing, it was a commonly heard request at Mardi Gras parades – and every night on Bourbon Street. During crowded weekends, for instance, the balconies along Bourbon would be packed with horny guys – and even more than a few gals, eager to take part in the action. As women of all colors, shapes, sizes, and ages strolled on the street below, the balcony hogheads would holler, "Show us your tits!" If a lady complied, the guys and gals would toss her a set of cheap plastic beads – made for pennies in China.

Every time I'd witnessed the all-too-familiar spectacle, I felt grateful Clare and I had never had any kids... at least none of the non-furry type.

As soon as the preppy dude propositioned the zombie chick, she closed the gap between them and, without preamble, bit a huge chunk of cloth-draped flesh from his shoulder. The consequence for offering her nothing in return – not even a cheap set of Carnival beads.

Releasing the lamppost and stumbling backward, he tried to push her away. From the look on his face, though, he'd barely felt the actual bite. He seemed too inebriated to register pain. Of course, when the zombie girl lunged toward him again and chomped off part of his nose, he seemed to notice that. With an anguished yelp, he crumpled onto the sidewalk and clutched his bloody face.

No matter what the girl did next, he was a gone pecan. So, I did the only reasonable thing I could: I sidestepped the ill-fated couple.

That's what you get, asshole.

Clare and I might've lived in the French Quarter – the place where the party had never seemed to end – but except for Halloween, we hadn't usually hung out in our own neighborhood. Naturally, we had our favorite bar – The Kerry Irish Pub, over on Decatur – but that cozy, music-filled joint had always been more popular with the locals.

For the most part, we'd stopped walking down Bourbon Street several years prior, before we'd even moved into our most recent apartment. We'd long had a distaste for the smelly, garish street, but our disgust increased the night we'd witnessed a large group of college-aged guys on a hotel balcony, tossing plastic beads at a girl who had collapsed on the sidewalk. Her friends had done nothing to help, so the assholes had just continued to hurl crappy necklaces at the poor young woman, vying to hit her in the head and cackling each time one of them scored. Like it was a righteous sport – or an innocent rite of passage in the Big Sleazy.

On second thought, maybe the world was better off with the zombies. Frankly, most of mankind sucked.

Beyond the Kerry, Clare and I had mainly stuck to the Marigny, the residential neighborhood adjacent to the Quarter. We were especially fond of the clubs on Frenchmen Street.

Goddammit, this sucks.

I would seriously miss the old-time jazz and blues music routinely blasting from The Spotted Cat and d.b.a., providing a rhythmic backdrop for the young dancers who often gathered in those clubs, twirling and twisting like colored feathers in the wind. On more than one occasion, Clare and I had promised each other we'd learn to dance like that, but perhaps knowing we'd never look as graceful had kept us from trying.

That and being a couple of old lazy asses.

Hey, most of those kids were just over twenty; we had an entire generation on them. Morbidly, I wondered how graceful the zombie versions of those dancers would seem now. Yeah, I'd really shown them: The graceless, overweight, old guy had endured among the zombies longer than most of the slender youngsters that once frequented Frenchmen Street.

Quite the victory.

Keeping an eye out for zombies, I turned onto St. Philip and, amid a smoky haze, promptly spotted a small group of people running for their lives down Bourbon Street, only a block away. I ducked behind an SUV, just as a horde of zombies, moving way too fast for my liking, chased after the free meal. Luckily, the walking dead (or, in that case, the running dead) and their victims were headed in the opposite direction from my destination, and once the path seemed clear, I resumed my trek across the French Quarter.

Someone familiar with the city's geography might ask why I was moving away from the parking lot on Rampart Street – where my ride out of Zombietown currently awaited me. Well, besides not leaving any guns in my apartment, I'd done something else pretty stupid.

Since I hadn't had enough money to buy all the shit I thought we would need during the impending apocalypse, I had applied for every high-interest credit card I could (all of which I'd happily never have to pay back). I'd also pawned Clare's maternal grandmother's wedding ring, given to my wife after her beloved grandmother had passed away – and like a real asshole, I hadn't told Clare.

Yep, I had to get that damn ring back before I headed out of town. Even if Clare preferred my safety over her grandmother's ring, I still wouldn't have felt right betraying my best friend and soulmate like that.

The pawn shop where I'd gotten eight grand for the ring was located in Mid-City, but I knew the owner, Troy Blanville (with whom I'd occasionally sipped beers at the Kerry), lived in the Quarter. I also knew he kept the ring at his house, not in the shop. I just hoped nothing had happened to him – or the ring – during the night.

As I neared the city's notorious party street, the smoke from nearby fires grew thicker and more pungent. Closer to the intersection, I realized flames engulfed several buildings on Bourbon, including my postal shop on one corner and Lafitte's Blacksmith Shop Bar on another.

For a moment, I paused to consider the irony: Lafitte's was one of only a handful of structures to have survived the Great Fires of the 18th century. Who could've guessed it would be a zombie apocalypse that finally destroyed it?

Many New Orleanians claimed the tavern had been haunted by two pirates said to have died after a bloody knife fight over a woman. Though a diehard horror nut, I'd never believed in ghosts. (Well, before recent events, I never would've believed in zombies either.) But, if the story about Lafitte's were true, I figured some pissed-off ghosts would soon be roaming the streets of the French Quarter, looking for a new place to haunt.

The fires were so intense I could feel them from the other side of the street; one look at Azazel's unhappy face told me she felt them, too. And for a kitty who could spend hours in front of my parents' fireplace up north, that was saying something.

So, after glancing to the southwest and watching as the herd of undead caught up with a few of the unlucky souls I'd seen running, I turned northeast and edged closer to my destination.

Understandably, there were even more corpses on Bourbon Street than I'd observed on St. Ann and Dauphine.

Most partyers must've congregated there before the first zombies arrived.

Having to leap over bodies made my journey tougher, but I still did my best to jog down the middle of the narrow street. If I encountered any zombies, I assumed it would be easier to dodge to one side or the other – and avoid getting trapped between cars and buildings.

I lifted the cat carrier and checked on Azazel: Now that we were keeping our distance from the flames, she seemed ready to go to sleep again.

Ah, to be a cat.

She'd even rolled onto her side (or maybe all my jiggling had knocked her over), enabling me to see the pronounced leopard spots covering her belly. They'd always made her look like one badass kitty.

Letting my mind wander a bit too long, I managed to run smack into another zombified businessman, which sent both Azazel and me to the ground. I landed hard on my ass, forcing my jaws to clamp shut and unleashing a jolt of pain through my torso that rivaled the headache. The axe promptly dropped from my hand, jabbing me in the crotch. At least I hadn't sliced my own balls off. The cat carrier, meanwhile, flew from my hands and tumbled end over end toward the gutter.

But, as luck would have it, the zombie dude had caught his suit jacket on the side-view mirror of somebody's piece-of-shit Toyota. So, I wasted no time getting to my feet, picking up poor Azazel's overturned carrier, and ensuring she was unharmed (if a tad disoriented and disgruntled) before quickly continuing down the street.

By the end of the block, though, I knew my cat and I were in serious trouble. I stood frozen at the intersection of Ursulines Avenue and Bourbon Street, not sure which way to go. In all four directions, I could see burning cars and buildings. Even worse, I spotted hundreds of zombies, shambling toward me from every direction, about to converge exactly where I stood.

I'd barely survived the first morning of the zombie apocalypse. I'd failed to escape the bloody, burning French Quarter, and I'd ultimately let my wife down. I was about to be devoured right there – and if not, Clare would likely kill me herself for endangering Azazel.

Chapter

10

"If we hole up, I wanna be somewhere familiar, I wanna know where the exits are, and I wanna be allowed to smoke." – Ed, *Shaun of the Dead* (2004)

"You crazy, boy?"

My head swiveled as I searched for the woman presumably talking to me. I recognized her as soon as my eyes landed on the dingy launderette on the northern corner of Ursulines and Bourbon. Myriam Beauvoir, a rotund black woman in her early sixties, stood in the wide-open doorway, beckoning me inside. Somehow, it didn't surprise me to see the joint was still intact and untouched by the nearby fires... although, as with every other building in the tightly packed Quarter, its preservation might not last long.

With a glance at the converging hordes, I calculated my shitty odds of survival and bolted through her front entrance. Once Azazel and I were safely inside the dimly lit washateria, Myriam closed and locked the glass door behind me – though a bit slower than I preferred.

I cautiously gazed around the place. Blinds covered all the windows. A musky, ginger-scented incense wafted through the air. Spaced across several old washers and dryers, half a dozen candles burned, which, beyond the sunshine spilling through the glass door, offered just enough light to make out most of the room.

As I focused my attention on the first zombies approaching the building, Myriam remained near the door, wordlessly removing a cigar from her shirt pocket, snipping off the end, and igniting it with a slender lighter. Years earlier, the local government had banned smoking in public places, but now that the zombie apocalypse had arrived, Myriam no longer had to slip outside for her daily cigar fix. Comforting to know a few silver linings had resulted from the end of the world.

She took a puff and exhaled a heady stream of smoke. "Idiot boy, why you runnin' 'round out dere?"

Wishing I hadn't packed all my own cigars in the van, I ignored her question and simply said, "You should get away from the door, Miss Myriam, or the zombies will see you."

She casually glanced over her shoulder, through the door, and pointed with her chin. "Da rosemary'll keep 'em away."

I traced her gaze to the two large, potted plants bookending the outer entrance. "The rosemary?" I stared at her as if she had lobster – or, more appropriately, crawfish – scrambling from her ears. "Rosemary, as in the herb?" I backed farther into the room, away from the easily breakable glass door.

She chuckled, shaking her head. "I told dat pretty wife uh yours you was no good." She took another satisfying puff on her cigar. "She shoulda listened to me."

Yes, it was true: Like my mother-in-law, Myriam had never approved of me – even though Clare and I had once been two of her most frequent customers. For nearly a decade, we'd used her launderette at least twice weekly, and while she'd legitimately liked Clare and merely tolerated my presence, she'd eventually banned me (and, by extension, my poor wife) from the premises.

Even now, I couldn't attribute the expulsion to one particular reason. Perhaps she'd grown weary of my repeated complaints about the dirty, unreliable condition of her machines. Maybe she didn't find my outlandish stories and controversial opinions as amusing as Clare did. Maybe, just maybe, she was still pissed about the time I'd snorted loudly after overhearing her conversation with a distraught woman – during which she'd revealed the fact that, as a voodoo priestess, she could easily remedy the woman's troubles with the no-good men of New Orleans.

OK, yeah, that's probably the moment she started hating me.

Regardless, I was no longer welcome in the launderette, which had ultimately led to our decision to install a small washer and dryer in our courtyard. Although Clare had grown to appreciate the convenient laundry setup, the situation hadn't initially pleased her. Never superstitious – or even religious, for that matter – she'd still considered it unwise to piss off the voodoo priestess who ran the only convenient washateria in the French Quarter. Used washers and dryers such as ours, bought from Tulane college kids, could break, after all.

Given what had happened between me and Myriam, I was just grateful she'd offered me sanctuary from the ravenous zombies outside. I couldn't kid myself, though. While she'd often been a generous soul to the ladies of the neighborhood, she likely wouldn't have come to my rescue if I hadn't been toting Azazel's carrier. Even she knew how much Clare adored the temperamental tabby – who, after her recent tumble in the street, had fallen asleep yet again.

I glanced from the carrier, still gripped in my left hand, to the glass door. The zombies outside had almost reached the entrance when the trio in front staggered to a halt, causing an almost comical traffic jam behind them. The three creatures gazed around the area in confusion and, bizarre as it might sound, lifted their noses in the air, as if sniffing something suspicious.

With their blood-stained faces, missing teeth, and swollen cheeks, eyes, and mouths, the three guys looked as if they'd endured a fifteen-round fight with an ogre, so it wasn't easy to discern subtle changes in their features. Still, their noses appeared to crinkle, as though they'd gotten a strong whiff of an intolerably foul smell, and the zombies behind them reacted in a similarly disgusted way. Seconds later, the crowd retreated from the launderette and lumbered elsewhere, likely searching for a more appetizing meal.

"Still doubt me?" Wearing an annoyingly smug expression, Myriam continued to puff on her cigar. "You see witcha own eyes."

"Holy crap."

"Damn beasts done broke troo da veil. Emptyin' d'Infernal into our realm," she murmured.

I had no clue what she was muttering about, but I didn't have the patience for some lengthy spiritual lesson. Besides, the goings-on outside fascinated me a lot more.

Although I couldn't really tell if the zombies had ultimately linked the bad smell to the rosemary plants, I still wanted to ask Myriam how she knew the herb would serve as such an effective undead repellent. But instead, I merely watched in amazement as the horde dispersed from the intersection.

With her demonstration done, Myriam ambled away from the door. "So, where's Clare?"

"Baton Rouge," I said, my focus drifting toward the *Employees Only* door near the cash register.

I wondered if the back area – which I knew doubled as a storage room and Myriam's tiny apartment – led to a side alley. All the times we'd gone there, I'd never noticed a pathway beside the building, but I figured it might be less conspicuous than waltzing out the front door. Especially if the zombies weren't as deterred as they'd seemed.

"At her mama's?"

"Yep." I turned toward her voice and noticed her rummaging through a satchel atop one of the dryers, the cigar resting in a small ashtray. "Say, Miss Myriam, does this place have a back door? I need to get to Governor Nicholls."

"No way out da back," she said, nodding toward the front entrance, "but it's almost clear enough out dere." Her point made, she returned to her feverish search.

I stepped toward her, curious about the hunt capturing her awareness.

Suddenly, her brown eyes brightened, and a satisfied smile spread across her round face. "Aha!" She pulled out three small baggies, each of which contained a fine grayish powder, though the candlelight made it hard to pinpoint the exact color. After turning toward me, she stepped closer, slid the baggies into the pocket of my long-sleeved shirt, and buttoned the flap.

I arched an eyebrow, suspicious of her intentions. "Probably not the best time to get high."

She shot me an aggravated look. "Not for puttin' up your nose, stupid. Dis dried frog powder." Perhaps reading my confused expression, she continued to explain. "Blow it onto a zombie, an' it can kill 'em. Might even take out more dan one. Even if you don't get it right in deir faces, it could at least hurt 'em. Give you time to get away."

"Frog powder, huh?"

OK, she might've been my savior, but she was still an eccentric old woman. Even after living in New Orleans for more than a decade, I had yet to meet a voodoo practitioner who'd convinced me of his or her powers.

Still, she'd been right about the zombies. They apparently hadn't approved of the rosemary plants, which, frankly, made me wish I had some of the miraculous herb to hang around the exterior of our step van. I considered asking Myriam for a few sprigs, but I didn't want to push my luck. She'd already been more generous than I had a right to expect, given our tumultuous history.

I turned toward the glass door. Even through the haze from the fires, the intersection seemed clear. Though wary to venture the three lengthy blocks that lay between Myriam's place and Troy Blanville's home, I couldn't waste any more time.

As if reading my thoughts, the voodoo priestess meandered to the door and threw the bolt.

"What about you, Miss Myriam? What's your plan?" I stepped closer to the entrance. "Maybe you should come with us."

She shook her head vehemently, her gray-tinged brown curls bouncing against her full cheeks. "Dis my home. No damn zombies gonna chase me off."

Just as stubborn as my neighbor Robert. Unwilling to let a thousand or more marauding zombies force her out. Admirable, perhaps, but the spreading flames would likely kill her before the undead could take their chance. Rosemary had a variety of uses, but as far as I knew, it wasn't known for extinguishing fire.

"You sure?"

She nodded. "I'm sure." She unleashed a toothy grin. "But I 'preciate da offer."

"Not a problem." I winked. "Bet Clare and I could use some voodoo mojo on the road."

She chuckled, her whole body trembling with mirth. "Bet you could, too."

As she opened the door, I stepped cautiously across the threshold, still gripping Azazel's carrier in one hand and my handy axe in the other. Glancing over my shoulder, I smiled at her.

"Thanks for helping me, Miss Myriam."

She shooed me away. "Jus' take care uh dat wife uh yours. She a keeper."

I smiled. "That she is." I hesitated, then said, "Good luck."

"You, too."

I took a few steps to the corner and surveyed both ends of Bourbon and Ursulines. Unfortunately, even through the smoky haze, I could see a massive amount of zombies still packed in three of the four directions – luckily, not the one I needed.

Taking one last look at Myriam, I noticed she had stepped outside to survey her part of the neighborhood. After apparently noting the three hordes of undead soon to converge at the intersection, she shifted her eyes to the corner, where I still stood like a catatonic platter of raw meat.

"Run, dummy," she said as she retreated inside and bolted the door.

Chapter

11

"No, please don't kill me, Mr. Ghostface. I wanna be in the sequel!" – Tatum Riley, *Scream* (1996)

Taking Myriam's advice, I bolted past the twenty-four-hour deli on the opposite corner. Known as the Quartermaster, it had long been my favorite spot for late-night munchies. Though one of the dirtiest joints in the neighborhood – where spotting roaches and rats scurrying along the baseboards wasn't uncommon – it had never looked so horrendous.

The weathered, glass-paneled doors barely hung from the hinges, and as I hurried past, I caught a glimpse of the decimated interior, with broken bottles, blood, brain matter, and intestines strewn across the dingy tiled floor and adorning the tightly packed shelves. That particular Halloween was probably one night the employees had wanted to close and lock their always-open doors.

Without stopping to see if I recognized any of the victims, I continued down Ursulines, toward the Mississippi River. I had to zigzag between the mutilated corpses and body parts on the asphalt – the cat carrier and go-bag banging against me as usual – but I covered the hazy, eerily quiet block in less than twenty seconds.

At Royal Street, I surveyed both directions, straining to see any movement through the smoke. Though I could still hear screams, gunshots, and other sounds of pandemonium all around me, I didn't see any zombies in the immediate vicinity.

It made me sad to think of all the cool historic homes, quaint inns, clever art galleries, and cluttered antique shops that lined Royal – and know they would either burn to the ground or become infested with the undead. There was nothing I could do to remedy the awful state of my old neighborhood, so I squelched the dismay, turned left, and headed toward Governor Nicholls Street.

As before, I jogged down the middle of the road, afraid of getting myself trapped against the buildings or between the parked cars, and as before, I did my best not to trip on the previous night's ill-fated revelers. If I were Robert or Myriam, I wouldn't have remained in the Quarter for lots of reasons – not the least of which was that, even if those who stayed managed to subdue the zombies and put out the fires, they would still need to remove all the carnage from the structures and the streets – or else, the neighborhood would look and smell like death for months to come.

I reached the corner of Royal and Governor Nicholls, where a three-story, dark gray structure towered over the intersection. Known by tourists and residents alike as the LaLaurie Mansion, it was an infamous, supposedly haunted home once owned by Nicolas Cage and frequently mentioned on the walking ghost tours that happened nightly.

Glancing at the bodies around me, I could tell at least three tour groups had been present when the zombie commotion had begun. Among the tattered, blood-stained costumes, I could still see some of the stickers the competing tour companies typically distributed to their paying customers.

What a terrible way for a cheesy ghost tour to end.

Turning right, I breathed a little more easily. So far, I hadn't encountered any undead, and I only had one block left to go.

Troy Blanville, my infrequent drinking buddy and the owner of several pawn shops, tacky souvenir emporiums, and strip clubs throughout the city, lived in one of several historic, multimillion-dollar homes in the Quarter. Actually, being the sleazy, over-the-top guy he was, he wouldn't have been satisfied with the usual fancy domicile, like the kind Brad Pitt and Angelina Jolie had famously owned many years before.

No, Troy had to possess one of the finest properties in the neighborhood and, as a bonus, piss off the wealthy New Orleans elite: the hoity-toity businessmen, philanthropists, society wives, professors, politicians, museum directors, and local celebrities who would never have welcomed him into their high-brow soirees. So, when the former owners of the Soniat House – three well-appointed townhouses built by a French sugar plantation owner in the 1830s – had decided to sell their business, Troy swooped in with the highest offer.

Situated at the western corner of Chartres and Governor Nicholls Streets, the former hotel included a couple adjacent buildings and two shady courtyards. In its heyday, it had been lauded as one of the most elegant hotels in New Orleans, boasting modern conveniences, gorgeous European fabrics and antiques, and all the classic architectural touches, from hanging gas lamps to wrought-iron grillwork on the galleries.

When Troy had gotten his hands on it, however, the place had undergone massive renovations. Eventually, it had reverted back to being a private home, complete with a sumptuous outdoor pool and an interior decorating design that could only be described as bordello chic.

As soon as I neared the peach-colored property on the corner, I suspected Troy was still alive. Normally, all the windows and doors on the multiple levels of the adjacent townhouses were exposed, but on that day, green shutters concealed almost all those facing Governor Nicholls, making them much harder for zombies and looters to breach. Topped with wrought-iron spikes, the concrete wall that protected the sides and rear of the property would also prove to be a challenging obstacle.

Though hard to tell with the shutters closed, it wouldn't have surprised me if his house still had power. He and I had discussed prepping on numerous occasions – even before I knew civilization was coming to an end. In fact, shortly after embarking on my doomsday prepping, I'd received plenty of solid advice from him.

Naturally, he hadn't believed me when I'd told him about the imminent zombie apocalypse, but ultimately, he hadn't really given a fuck about the specific reason for Armageddon. Whether solar flares, volcanoes, comets, or other unstoppable disasters came to pass, Troy – that resourceful, morally challenged bastard – would be prepared for the end of life as we knew it.

I'd almost reached the side door of Troy's complex when I noticed a man careening around the corner, from the front of the property on Chartres. Dressed like a doctor for Halloween, he looked as though he'd seen much better days, and I suspected it wasn't expert make-up that had resulted in his horrific appearance.

Huge gashes marred his face, so deep I could see his teeth through his cheeks. One eye was missing from its socket, and a broomstick protruded from his chest. Yep, someone had jammed a broken broom handle deep into his rib cage. It apparently hadn't slowed him down, but I figured it would offer me a bit of leverage.

Moaning loudly, he lunged toward me. To prevent an untimely impaling, I dropped my axe and poor Azazel's carrier and pushed against the handle. The far end must've been lodged against his spine because it stayed firmly in place, which helped me to keep the zombie at bay.

Azazel, meanwhile, caterwauled from somewhere behind me. No matter where or how her carrier had landed, she was understandably one unhappy feline. I felt bad for her, of course, but while tussling with the latest threat, I didn't have time to soothe her.

Even with the handle jutting awkwardly from his body, the zombified doctor managed to tackle me to the ground, the contents of my go-bag jabbing me in the back. Although his weight almost knocked the wind from me, he'd fortunately landed on his side, so the broomstick failed to impale me. Before his teeth had reached my exposed neck – or I'd passed out from the rotten smell emanating from him – I pushed the handle upward, turning him away in the process, and scurried from beneath him.

After scrambling to my feet and retrieving my axe, I thought about chopping into the zombie's head, but I knew I'd be in trouble if the weapon got stuck in his skull. Particularly since I'd spotted a trio of zombified teenagers headed my way, from farther down Governor Nicholls.

By the time I'd picked up Azazel's carrier – which had, once again, landed upside-down – the zombie doctor had risen to his feet. As his white coat fell open, I noticed an enormous hole in his stomach, from which poured a green-tinged black goo – the likely source of the awful smell that almost overpowered the ever-present burning odor in the air.

With my back facing Troy's complex, I surveyed the immediate area and retreated toward the side entrance. Four zombies were converging on my position, so while I kept an eye on them, I used my axe-wielding hand to ring the doorbell and rattle the outer gate. Luckily, the zombified doctor slipped in his own gore and landed on his ass.

At that moment, I heard a hearty bellow from above me. Looking up, I noticed Troy on his second-floor balcony. Framed by the vibrant foliage hanging from the ceiling and along the iron railing, the large black man was, not surprisingly, wearing his uniform of choice: a red-and-black smoking jacket that made him look like an overweight, dark-skinned Hugh Hefner. He was also staring directly at me, grinning like a hyena.

"Well, well, well, if it isn't my old pal Joe Daniels. The man who predicted this whole mess." He chuckled. "Good to see you're alive and well, my friend."

I glanced at the struggling doctor and the three approaching teens, then back at Troy. "Yeah, well, if you don't open this fucking door, I might not last much longer."

Chapter

12

"You play a good game, boy... but the game is finished. Now you die." – The Tall Man, Phantasm (1979)

Troy chuckled again. "Looks like you're in quite a pickle." Some distant movement must've caught his eye because his gaze shifted beyond me, and his shit-eating grin quickly faded.

I turned to trace his worried glance and spotted a sizable group of zombies ambling amid the smoky haze between the LaLaurie Mansion and Troy's ostentatious home.

Snapping my head back to the gallery, I shouted, "Enough bullshit! Just get down here and open the fucking door."

"Down in a sec." He turned and vanished around the corner, presumably headed back to an open doorway along the front gallery.

While I waited for my questionable savior, I refocused on my present dilemma. With every passing minute, the two converging groups of zombies were getting closer, but the doctor still posed the most immediate threat. He'd finally managed to regain his footing and bypass his innards without slipping onto his ass again.

I had to give him kudos: He was one determined fucker. He lunged toward me, but even with the cat carrier in one hand and the axe in the other, I was still able to push him backward, using the broken handle as a lever.

After repeating the same tiresome dance a few times, I finally squeezed the axe behind my belt and clutched the broomstick. The zombie tried to swipe at me, but luckily, the splintered handle was longer than his reach.

Naturally, the insanity couldn't last forever. Soon, at least a dozen zombies would have me and Azazel pinned against Troy's courtyard wall – with no exit in sight. With mere seconds to spare, I calculated the odds of my evading the undead – abandoning Clare's ring in the process – before I became hopelessly trapped.

My cat seemed to sense our impending demise, too, as she'd begun hissing at the approaching zombies – and probably wondering why the hell her daddy had endangered her in such a ridiculous way. In fact, her furry face had just turned to hiss at me when I heard several locks click and the wooden door creak open behind me, followed by the gate.

Suddenly, I felt a meaty hand grab my shirt and yank me backward, almost making me lose my grip on the carrier. If I dropped Azazel in a mess of zombies, I might as well let them take me, too – because Clare would never forgive me.

"Get your ass in here," Troy growled.

I shoved the broomstick as hard as I could, propelling the zombified doctor into the trio of undead teenagers. All four creatures toppled to the sidewalk as I stumbled backward into the well-lit foyer. As the working doorbell had already indicated, Troy definitely had electricity, no doubt powered by the various concealed generators on his property.

While I steadied myself and tried to soothe Azazel with a few choice words, Troy slammed the gate, closed the door, and engaged the assorted locks and bolts. Then, he whipped around, raised a rather menacing .44 Magnum revolver, and pointed the barrel at my head. My heart rate, which had quickened outside at the thought of my imminent death by zombies, sped up even more.

Instinctively, I stepped backward and shifted Azazel's carrier behind me, which didn't prevent her from hissing and growling with disapproval. Hopefully on my behalf.

I stared coldly at Troy, wondering how a supposed friend could turn on me – especially during a zombie apocalypse. "What the fuck are you doing?"

Troy's eyes traced my frame – certainly a bloody, goopy mess – but the sad truth was none of the blood belonged to me.

"Have you been bitten?" he asked, his tone both fretful and reluctant.

Ah, of course.

I'd seen enough zombie flicks to know he was concerned about the infection spreading inside his sanctuary.

"No, man, I'm clean. None of this blood is mine." I cocked my head, listening to Azazel's subdued growl. "Would you please lower the gun? You're freakin' my cat out."

He hesitated for only a moment, then dropped the

gun-wielding hand to his side. "Sorry, kid. Had to be sure."
Troy called everyone "kid" – and even though he only had
five years on me, he'd always seemed much older – like a
black version of Marlon Brando from the first *Godfather*.

My heart rate began to normalize, and I shifted
Azazel's carrier back to my side. As stressful as it was to have
a loaded gun aimed at you – something I'd unfortunately
experienced a few times in crime-ridden New Orleans – I
supposed I should've felt lucky. Troy could've chosen to test
me outside, with a dozen zombies closing in for the kill.
Quite neighborly of him to invite me indoors before
threatening to shoot me.

Sensing movement to my right, I turned and noticed a
handful of gorgeous twentysomething women, lounging
around the plush, red-hued living room, all in various states
of undress.

*The entire world's ending out there, and this guy
decides to host a goddamn orgy.*

Troy himself would've won no beauty prizes. A
balding, fifty-year-old lush, he had to weigh more than three
hundred pounds. The babes presently relaxing in his living
room – and probably elsewhere in the sprawling mansion –

were there because they believed Troy could protect them. Plain and simple.

A voluptuous brunette, wearing a thin lacy number, winked at me, and I turned back to my friend. "Having a party?"

A slender redhead, sporting high-heeled sandals and a white string bikini, rose from one of the brocade sofas and sauntered across the foyer. As she passed Troy, he smacked her ass, eliciting a girlish giggle.

He winked at me, tucking the Magnum in a side pocket of his smoking jacket. "If the world's gotta end, might as well go out in style. Or at least getting a great piece of tail."

"Well put," I said.

Just then, I sensed a throbbing pain in my left wrist and realized I'd been lugging Azazel for a while. At thirteen pounds, she might be a reasonable size for a cat, but still, she was heavier than the average bowling ball – and my arm likely would've hurt if I'd been running around the neighborhood with one of those in tow, too.

I set her carrier on the marble floor. As soon as I did, a few of the girls rushed toward me to coo over the cute tabby. After giving them the requisite warning that Azazel could be more vicious – or at least less sociable – than she seemed, I faced Troy again. It was time to get what I'd come for.

Beating me to the punch, he said, "So, what are you doing here, kid? Figured you'd be halfway to Michigan by now."

"I need to get it back," I replied, more sheepishly than I'd intended.

His brow furrowed, as if he needed to process what it was. Then, his eyes widened, and he expelled a guffaw. "Are you fucking kidding me? You fought your way across this bloody nightmare, just to get a goddamn ring?!"

Yeah, I felt pretty stupid for risking my life – and Azazel's – over a now-worthless trinket, but I wanted to make sure Clare had her grandmother's ring. Cuz, no matter what happened out there on the road, I doubted we'd return to New Orleans anytime soon. In short, when it came to securing the ring or any other memorabilia, it was now or never.

Troy didn't really require an explanation – he was simply curious – so in answer to his question, I merely said, "Yep."

He just stared at me for a few seconds, then shook his head in disbelief. For once, words seemed to have failed him. In fact, it wasn't until a topless blonde asked him for some more blow that he finally snapped out of his temporary fugue.

Turning to me, he said, "To be honest, I often wish I had one of those tear gas grenades you bought." He sighed, sounding rather tired of his high-maintenance playmates. "Just clear them all out."

I shrugged. "Yeah, but the gas is kind of a waste. Won't be much good against zombies."

"Maybe not," he agreed. "But I sure could use some peace and quiet." Keeping his eyes on me, he gently pushed the girl aside. "As for the ring... I been storing it in my bedroom."

Without waiting for a response, he headed toward the nearest staircase and signaled for me to follow him. At the bottom of the stairs, he hesitated. "Just don't touch anything, OK? That shit all over your clothes might be contagious."

Reluctantly, I left Azazel downstairs. Clare would've scolded me for leaving her alone with a bunch of strangers, but I trusted my ferocious tiger could handle herself. Besides, Azazel would surely appreciate sitting still for a little while – and my sore arm definitely needed a break. Before walking away, I urged her to refrain from biting the three nearly naked women kneeling around her carrier, who were arguing over who should be able to pet her first.

As I trailed Troy upstairs, I couldn't help but chuckle.

Maybe they'll leave her alone after she bites the first one who sticks her hand in the carrier.

Chapter

13

"You'll forgive me if I don't stay around to watch. I just can't cope with the freaky stuff." – Barry Convex, *Videodrome* (1983)

Troy had purchased the former Soniat House for more than twelve million dollars, and though the buildings that made up his complex were roughly two hundred years old, he'd opted for a less traditional decor. In the end, he'd created a tacky, outlandish oasis Larry Flynt might've been proud to call home.

Inviting sofas and lounges peppered every room, even the kitchen. Every bedroom boasted a stripper pole, sex swing, or other X-rated enhancement, not to mention the requisite dildos and assorted adult toys. The walls, curtains, and furniture primarily came in varied shades of red and purple, such as the violet-hued velvet wallpaper lining the grand staircase.

Sensual photographs, paintings, sculptures, and sconces covered nearly every mantle, shelf, table, and surface in sight – and the scenes didn't just depict tasteful nudes. They showcased people fucking in every way imaginable.

Overall, the place reminded me of the House of the Rising Sun, the former brothel that now occupied the upper floors of my landlord's property management office on St. Louis Street. Only, the brothel was infinitely classier.

"Think you might've overdone the decor, Troy?"

He chuckled. "No offense, but I'm not gonna take decorating advice from a sentimental dummy who just fought through herds of zombies for a lousy diamond ring." Pausing at the top of the staircase, he glanced at a four-foot-tall marble statue of a nude woman squatting over a naked man, apparently peeing on his chest. "OK, yeah. I see your point."

We shared a momentary chuckle – a welcome break from the stress and fear that had been coursing through my veins. As the laughter faded, we continued down the seductively lit hallway, past open doors revealing other tempting young ladies.

Troy certainly didn't discriminate: He liked women of all shapes, sizes, and ethnicities. From petite and skinny to tall and enormous, most women were gorgeous in his eyes, and he'd always claimed any lady could be fun in bed – especially if her partner knew what he was doing.

Eventually, we entered the master bedroom suite. Right away, I spotted a completely naked, large-breasted brunette lying across – I kid you not – a round, ten-foot-wide bed, like the kind you used to see in those old porn films. Clearly comfortable with her nude body, the woman barely glanced at us as we made a beeline for the antique mahogany wardrobe in one corner of the bedroom.

Without even acknowledging the naked chick, Troy opened the ornate doors of the wardrobe, slid out a bottom drawer, and peered inside. After shuffling through some silk shirts, he sighed heavily and finally glanced toward the bed. "Lily, where's all the jewelry I had in here?"

Pointedly ignoring him, the so-called Lily (an innocent name for a not-so-innocent girl) picked up a bottle of dark red nail polish from the nightstand and started nonchalantly painting the fingernails of her left hand.

Troy slammed the drawer shut and stomped toward the bed. "I said... where the fuck is all the jewelry I kept in that drawer?"

She concentrated on glossing her left thumbnail. "The girls are wearing most of it."

Troy grunted in disgust. "I told y'all to stay outta my wardrobe!"

With a petulant sigh, she finally stopped polishing her nails and shot him an exasperated look. "We were bored," she whined. "Thought a treasure hunt would cheer us up."

A sudden sparkle made me examine her left hand more closely.

Fuck. This chick is actually wearing Clare's ring.

I moved closer to the bed. "Hey, where'd you get that?"

"What, this?" Biting her lip, she held out her left hand and glanced at the twinkling diamond. "Found it." She gazed at me with her heavily shaded bedroom eyes. "You like?"

Troy shook his head, understandably annoyed at his sexy playmate. "Jesus, Lily. Give it to me."

She pulled herself into a sitting position, yanked the red silk sheet over her body, crossed her arms, and pouted. Even mostly covered, the girl was stunning. Troy might have to endure some immature bullshit from his slutty house guests, but he'd still die a happy man.

"Hand it over," he said, stepping toward her and holding out his palm. "Now."

"Why should I?" she asked defiantly.

He snapped his fingers and extended his palm again. "Cuz this guy..." he said, gesturing toward me with his other hand, "...had to walk through a whole lotta zombie guts to come all the way here and get that goddamn ring. It belonged to his wife's grandmother, for fuck's sake."

She gazed at my stained clothes and crinkled her pert nose – apparently noting the blood and other nasty fluids she'd ignored before that moment. Then, she unfurled her left hand and appraised the ring in question: a sizable two-carat diamond, encircled by tiny garnets.

Clare, who typically wore less expensive jewelry, had only donned the flashy ring whenever we attended a garish holiday event, outrageous Mardi Gras ball, or fancy Halloween party, where dressing to the nines was required.

She loved the ring not for its monetary value, but because it had belonged to a grandmother she'd been very close to.

A precious heirloom presently twirling around the finger of a big-breasted stripper. Despite my wife's raunchy sense of humor, such a scene would not have amused her. And I couldn't really blame her.

With a melodramatic sigh, Lily reluctantly removed the ring from her slender finger and dropped it onto Troy's open hand, letting the sheet fall, exposing her rather remarkable breasts – a manipulative move she'd probably used to her advantage in whichever strip joint she'd worked. "Did he at least pay you what he owes you?"

I glanced sheepishly at Troy. I didn't have the cash, and he knew it. But the end of the world had come, and money no longer meant a thing to him. To any of us.

"He's a friend," he said, placing the ring inside my cupped hand. "Besides, he gave me a heads-up about the zombies. I owe him at least one for that."

I slipped the ring into the small coin pocket of my jeans. "Thanks, man." Then, I scratched my head awkwardly, hesitating to ask the other question on my mind.

Again, he seemed to sense my discomfort. "So, what else did you come for? Food? Water? Booze? Got quite a spread in the dining room."

I grimaced. Yes, my stomach had grumbled all morning, and my throat was parched as hell. No, two granola bars and two aspirin hadn't provided enough pain-free energy for a death-defying sprint through the French Quarter. And sure, I could've killed someone for a gin and tonic. But at that precise moment, I had only one priority: keeping myself alive long enough to reach Clare, and hopefully for a while into the future.

"Do you, by any chance," I asked, "have a spare gun I could borrow?" I knew Troy – paranoid fucker that he was – had quite a few firearms in the house, but whether he'd give me a piece was another story. He likely doubted I'd ever be back to return it.

Troy's brow furrowed. "What the fuck happened to the arsenal you bought?"

Feeling stupid all over again, I gazed down at my sneakers. Now covered in zombie goo. So much for changing my shoes. Or my clothes.

Eh, fuck it.

Given any luck, I'd have time to clean up later.

With renewed purpose, I met Troy's eyes, which glimmered with wry amusement. "I packed it all in my rig."

In truth, I thought I'd be safe for a few more days. "Didn't expect the zombies so soon. All I had left in my apartment were a few steak knives and this axe." I plucked the weapon from behind my belt.

He shook his head, likely wondering how such an idiot had survived so long. "You're killing me, kid," he said, then, with a chuckle, returned to the wardrobe, where he proceeded to rummage through a different drawer. Apparently full of underwear: for men and women alike.

Eventually, he pulled out a derringer: an antique, double-barreled palm pistol that surely wouldn't be good for more than two shots at a time. It was no Magnum revolver, but beggars like me certainly couldn't afford to be choosy. Or ungrateful.

After handing me the gun, he returned to the drawer and dug through an assortment of boxers, bras, panties, and lingerie until he located a box of .38 bullets.

I set my backpack on a small mahogany table featuring yet another tacky, X-rated sculpture, stuffed some of the bullets into the front pockets of my jeans, and packed the rest of the ammo in the bag. I slipped the axe into an easily accessible side pocket and, following a much-needed swig from one of the water bottles in my backpack, carefully loaded the derringer.

"Takes .38 bullets," I mused. "Thought derringers were all .22 caliber?"

"Nah," Troy replied. "They even make a .45."

I zipped up my satchel and resecured it on my back. "Thanks again, man." I held up the gun with one hand and tapped the coin pocket with the other. "For both."

He laughed. "Happy to help. I figure, this way, if you manage to make it back to Clare, you won't have to go through a divorce on top of everything else."

"Yeah," Lily piped up from the bed, "cuz if you were my man, and you pawned my diamond ring, I would definitely dump your ass."

"Even if it was to buy a bunch of guns to protect *your* ass?" Not sure why I took the bait. Just felt like arguing with someone.

She smiled coquettishly. "Yep. Even then."

I shrugged. Deep down, I knew Clare would much prefer an arsenal over a diamond ring, even one that had once belonged to her beloved grandmother. Pissed as she might be to learn I'd pawned the ring without telling her, she certainly wouldn't divorce me over one well-intended transgression.

Practical as she often was, she'd probably be more likely to leave me for putting my life – and Azazel's – in mortal peril over a piece of now-worthless jewelry. Yet another reason why I'd rather be married to her, my soulmate, than the big-breasted pain in the ass on the bed.

"From now on, Lily," Troy warned, "stay outta my shit. Or I might just have to dump *your* ass on the street."

Leaving Lily in full-on pout mode, Troy and I exited the suite and retraced our steps down the hallway and staircase.

On the lower level, he turned to me, an unusually worried look in his eyes. "So, what's it like out there? I've seen some of the carnage from the galleries, and heard the yelling, but is it as insane as it seems?"

"Worse. There are dead bodies everywhere. And real people still fighting. And screaming. And dying." I swallowed, struggling to forget some of the awful shit I'd seen. "If I were you, I wouldn't stay here long."

"Why?" He gazed around the adult playground he'd created for himself, then looked back at me, a weary expression on his face. "Got everything I need here."

"Maybe so. But, Troy, your supplies won't last forever. Neither will the plumbing. And honestly, there are several fires raging through the Quarter. Your block might be OK for now, but if no one's around to stop them, it'll just take one good breeze... and the flames'll be hopping from street to street."

His expression turned pensive, but he didn't say anything.

"Besides," I continued, "as wonderful as it might seem to have a bunch of sexy babes around, you might've done better by hiring some armed guards. And building a few more booby traps. The zombies might eventually find a way inside, you know, and if not them, you'll still have to worry about looters."

He nodded sagely. "All good points." He smirked. "Even with your warning, I admit the whole zombie thing took me by surprise... but I certainly won't go down without a fight."

I grinned. "I'm sure you won't."

"So, what're you gonna do?"

"Well, Clare's in Baton Rouge. At her mom's place. So, I'm gonna drive there, grab the two of them, and follow through with the plan."

His brow furrowed. Again. "Joe, I've been listening to the shortwave. This is happening all over the country. Really think you can make it all the way up to Michigan?"

I shrugged. "Don't know, but I gotta at least try."

"How can you even be sure the roads'll be clear? They're probably more jammed up than during a hurricane evacuation."

"What evacuation? I don't remember an official warning on the news. The whole thing just spread like wildfire through the neighborhood. Probably the city, too. In one night. How many people you think made it out?"

Troy sighed. Holed up in his sex palace, listening to the shortwave, he likely had fewer answers than I did.

By the time I'd made a pit stop in one of his gold-trimmed bathrooms, retrieved Azazel's carrier, and followed my friend to the front door facing Chartres Street, I had seen at least another half-dozen girls. I took back my original assessment: Larry Flynt would've looked up to the guy.

Troy smiled sheepishly as yet another hot, barely dressed chick sauntered across the spacious foyer. "Sure you don't wanna stay?"

If I confessed it crossed my mind, even for a second, I'd seem like a giant dick, but honestly, the thought never occurred to me. I needed Clare more than ever before, and nothing would stop me from getting to her.

With his Magnum revolver at the ready, Troy carefully opened the front door, unlatched the shutter, and peered out into the smoky street. When he seemed sure it was clear of the undead, he retreated from the doorway. "Good luck, kid."

"Same to you," I whispered as I stepped onto the

sidewalk.

I heard the shutter softly close behind me. Then, following a quick glance in both directions, I headed southwest on Chartres – away from the zombies that might still be lingering by Troy's side door – and left my friend's ill-fated house of pleasure behind.

Chapter

14

"In a world where the dead are returning to life, the word 'trouble' loses much of its meaning." – Kaufman, *Land of the Dead* (2005)

That part of Chartres was usually quiet and less traveled than Bourbon at night, but the prior day had been Halloween, one of the French Quarter's most crowded days of the year. So, it didn't surprise me to see bodies – and unsightly pieces of bodies – strewn across the bloody asphalt. As usual, I had to play a horror-show version of hopscotch to traverse the block, all while awkwardly toting a backpack and a cat carrier and bypassing any solitary zombies meandering through the haze.

If not for that, though, and the pervasive scent of smoke mixed with the rancid odor of rotting flesh, it would've been an ideal autumn day for a walk through the neighborhood. Sunny, cool, with refreshing breezes drifting from the Mississippi River, which lay a couple blocks to my left. I'd often traveled along that particular stretch, between the well-maintained Beauregard-Keyes House and the Old Ursuline Convent, on my daily walks – and as with everything else in the Quarter, I sure would miss it.

At the corner, I turned right onto Ursulines, and my brief lucky streak ended. I had to cross five more blocks to reach the parking lot where I'd stored the van, and based on the number of zombies in the area, it wouldn't be an easy feat.

True, the streets weren't teeming with as many undead creatures as I'd expected. While preparing for the world-ending disaster, I'd imagined the roadways of New Orleans resembling a carnivalesque crowd of wall-to-wall zombies, and though I'd already observed a ton of them, some even traveling in large packs, there were nowhere near the numbers I'd anticipated. Perhaps I'd failed to account for all the devoured people lying in the streets.

Farther down Ursulines, toward the river, I'd spotted a group of undead revelers. Unfortunately, a few of them had spotted me, too, but as they stumbled beneath the overhanging galleries, I realized they were too far behind to promise much trouble. At least for me and Azazel.

The problem for us lay ahead: varied packs of zombies wandering through the nebulous atmosphere, exactly in the direction I was headed.

Still moving forward, I lifted the carrier and eyed my cat. "Alright, Azazel, get ready for a bumpy ride."

Once again, she didn't seem pleased. In fact, she was still growling. I tried blinking tenderly at her, which usually soothed her, but the calm, sleepy demeanor from earlier in the day had vanished. Chased away by her sickening tumbles, the broomstick-wielding zombie, and everything else she'd endured in the last few hours.

Like me, she probably just wanted to get the fuck out of New Orleans. Like me, she probably longed to see Clare again.

I lowered the carrier and glanced up and down the block. The zombies behind me were still headed my way, so I picked up the pace. Although survival was uppermost on my mind, I couldn't help but notice the familiar landmarks as I hurried past them: the kumquat trees Clare and I had often raided, the patisserie where we'd spent many tranquil, high-calorie mornings, and all the historic homes and inns that made the Quarter so unique.

During the decade or so I'd called the Big Easy home, each one of those structures had left a permanent mark on my brain. Almost every day, even during rainstorms, I would walk through the Quarter and the hipper, artsier Marigny, and I'd often note the medley of curious architecture that made up New Orleans, from Caribbean-style bungalows and double-shotgun homes to ornate, multistory European townhouses. I especially favored the gorgeous, Spanish-style wrought-iron railings that bordered most of the balconies and galleries in the Quarter, many of which supported a cornucopia of hanging vines, plants, and flowers.

Admittedly, as beautiful and sweet-smelling as they were, I'd often cursed those very same plants on my daily walks. Mainly because the tenants and homeowners always seemed to pick the most inopportune moments to water the foliage, frequently showering me with cold water as I trekked below.

Damn it.

The momentary daydream dissipated as I realized I was once again being sprinkled from above. Glancing upward, in search of rain or dripping flowers, I acknowledged the sickening truth: It wasn't water, but blood, raining down on me from a second-floor balcony, where a female zombie was devouring the innards of her soon-to-be zombie mate.

Way to kill the fond memory.

After ensuring no infected blood had landed on Azazel's carrier, I continued toward the intersection of Ursulines and Royal, where a private walled compound sat on one corner, a cleverly disguised parking garage on another, and a vintage pharmacy on the third. From the fourth, I suddenly heard a familiar blues riff, cranked up louder than it should've been. The three-story brick home on the western corner of the intersection had long been one of my favorites in the Quarter, complete with gas lamps, hanging greenery, iron grillwork, and a set of double doors on the lower level painted an eye-popping shade of red.

Until a few years before, the impressive, 19th-century home had only had two floors, but following an extensive renovation amazingly approved by the hard-ass Vieux Carré Commission, it now boasted three levels.

A beer bottle crashed to the asphalt in front of me, and I gazed at the wraparound gallery on the second floor, which was filled to capacity with young, drunken revelers, all dancing, hollering, and basically being typical New Orleanians. Yep, they were partying during a zombie apocalypse.

Well, it is the Big Easy.

Glancing up Royal Street, I noticed a herd of perhaps a hundred zombies stumbling toward me – or, rather, the music. In the other direction, I could see a group twice that size headed my way. Behind me, the number of zombie followers had grown, and just ahead, my route toward the parking lot also appeared to be blocked. While the normally soothing sounds of Tab Benoit's "Medicine" vibrated the floorboards overhead, countless zombies continued to surround me and Azazel, leaving no clear route to our destination.

"Hey, dude, what the hell you doin' down there?" a scraggly-haired kid in his twenties shouted from the balcony.

Before I could answer, a young, red-haired woman,

wearing a kaleidoscopic gown fit for a Mardi Gras ball, leaned over the railing and eyed me warily. "Whatcha got in the carrier?"

"My cat," I replied as I glanced in each direction, still hoping to conjure up a doable exit plan.

"Aww..." she cooed. "Can I see him?"

Realizing the only viable escape route would involve entering one of the nearby buildings, I looked up at the girl and shouted, "If you let me in, I would be happy to show *her* to you!"

She promptly disappeared into the dancing crowd, and I stepped closer to the corner, trusting her vanishing act meant she'd headed downstairs to let me in. I turned my back toward the double front doors and surveyed all four directions, just as the first zombie stepped within shooting distance. Actually, it was two zombies, connected at the torso.

"Holy crap," I said to no one in particular. "That's an awesome costume."

Before an inconvenient apocalypse had crashed the city's annual Halloween celebration, the couple had obviously taken a lot of care with the joint outfit. Both painted in silver from head to toe and featuring a medley of faces and limbs, the man and woman resembled the T-1000 from *Terminator 2* (a kickass movie from the early 1990s). Specifically, they looked like the melting version at the climax of the film – when the cleaved, metallic villain tumbles into a pit of molten steel and morphs into all the bodies it's previously copied.

The two revelers had assembled one of the coolest creations I'd ever seen – and the blood and gore only added to the chilling effect. Honestly, even though someone had bitten off the lady's nose, and the guy was missing an entire arm, they still could've won the top prize at a Halloween costume contest.

Of course, their killer costume presented an added benefit: Even after the turmoil of being eaten by and turned into zombies, they were still sewn together via their silver bodysuits, which made it easier for me to swing them around and off balance.

"Woah," someone shouted from above. "What a cool fucking costume!"

Shit. Shit. Shit!

The peanut gallery had spotted the couple. Worse, all the stoned, drunk, ridiculous partyers cared more about how amazing the zombies looked than the fact that they were fucking zombies – and Azazel and I were once again in danger.

Remember how I said most of humanity sucked?

Just then, in an explicable feat of coordination (or muscle memory), the linked zombies righted themselves and headed directly for me. At that moment, I made the decision to pocket the untested derringer and retrieve my trusty axe from the mesh side pouch on my backpack. Even as I sidestepped the three zombie arms grasping for me, the partygoers above started booing me, as if finally comprehending how I intended to use the weapon gripped in my right hand.

"Leave 'em alone," some idiot yelled. "They never hurt nobody!"

"Please don't kill 'em, mister," another moron hollered.

"I think they're already dead," I shouted in response.

"You don't have to be so negative, dude," yet another voice piped up.

"Jesus, give it a rest," I grumbled.

While it did seem a bit sacrilegious to slay the poor unfortunate undead to the remarkable sounds of one of my favorite blues guitarists, I felt certain Tab – if he were still alive – would understand. Survival, in the end, trumped artistic respect.

Taking an overdue peek at the streets around me, I figured the *T2* couple wasn't my only problem. The zombie hordes were closing in quickly, the front doors of the party house remained closed, and I had run out of time. Suddenly, camping out at Troy's palace of pleasure didn't seem so intolerable after all.

I spun the *T2* couple around again. Just as before, the zombies couldn't keep their balance, but when the guy stumbled to his knees, yanking his noseless counterpart with him, I took the opportunity to bring my axe down onto the guy's skull. Not sure what to blame – my anger at the inebriated idiots above me, the renewed energy Tab Benoit's rocking blues always gave me, or the couple's accelerated decomposition due to the zombie virus – but my decorative axe split the man's head open like a rotten cantaloupe, almost to the bridge of his nose. His morphing days were over.

Luckily, the axe didn't get stuck (as it had during my first kill with the weapon). I rolled the guy backward onto the ground, in a supine position, so I could more easily put down the woman. Raising the axe above my head, I realized I had yet to kill a female zombie.

But hey, there's a first time for everything.

Before I could unleash my swing, though, I heard a creaking sound in front of me, barely discernible amid the pulsating music.

Looking up, I noticed one of the red doors of the party house was wide open. The gown-wearing girl who'd wanted to see Azazel up close and personal stood in the doorway, a stoned yet horrified expression on her pretty face. Clearly, she had no intention of watching me chop the woman's skull to smithereens, so before she could change her mind about inviting me inside, I lowered the axe, tightened my grip on Azazel's carrier, and bolted toward the open doorway. Not so gently, I pushed the girl backward into the foyer, slammed the door with a resounding thud, and threw the deadbolt.

Then, I closed my eyes and remembered to breathe again.

Chapter

15

"Meat's meat, and a man's gotta eat." – Vincent Smith, *Motel Hell* (1980)

Once my breathing had steadied, I peeked through the blinds covering the nearest window in the shadowy foyer. The female half of the undead T-1000 was still lying on the pavement, repeatedly trying to tug herself upward, but apparently encountering too much resistance from the dead weight beside her. With her limited zombie brain, she just couldn't figure out why she was unable to detach herself and rise to her feet.

The scene might've been comical if not for the fact that the six zombies following me down Ursulines had finally entered the intersection and were now headed for the red double doors like missiles in search of a bull's-eye.

I'd almost forgotten the stoned redhead behind me when she finally found her voice.

"You were about to hit that woman with an axe," she said, her tone incredulous.

I turned to face her. "Um, yeah, she's a zombie. If you don't put 'em down, they'll rip you apart or turn you into one of them. A mindless cannibal."

She shook her head slowly, disapproval in her eyes. "You're not supposed to ever hit a woman."

Was the girl simply stoned out of her gourd? Or would she have labeled me a misogynist or a domestic abuser even if she'd been completely sober?

"I'm an equal-opportunity zombie killer." I smirked. "Or just think of me as a feminist. If it's good enough for a male zombie, it's good enough for a female."

She cocked her head and stared at me for several seconds before finally nodding. "Cool... well, welcome to our party." She squinted at me. "So, what are you supposed to be? A zombie?"

I glanced down at my blood-splattered clothes and the equally gory axe. "Uh, yeah, right. This is just a costume."

"Cool." Grinning, she turned away from me and wandered into the living room, where several costumed people were milling about, lounging on sofas, or getting high.

Peering through the blinds again, I saw the zombie hordes had converged. Seven zombies had now become hundreds, maybe even thousands. And all of them seemed to want an invitation to the party.

Even with the amplified music reverberating throughout the house, the thuds and grunts loudened against the front doors, and I wondered how long the solid wooden barrier would hold. My only consolation: I hadn't lured the zombies to the drunken smorgasbord. The blues had done the job for me.

After a moment, during which I weighed and tossed aside my limited options, I turned to find the redhead waiting for me at the bottom of the nearest staircase. Glancing through the slits of the carrier, I could see Azazel's green eyes fixed on my face, as if willing me to make a decision. So, with a shrug, I opted to follow the girl upstairs.

I doubted anyone there would be useful in a zombie fight – or sober enough to survive one – but I certainly couldn't leave the way I'd come. And maybe I'd locate a back exit before the ravenous zombies managed to beat down the front doors.

For the moment, I tried to appreciate the fact that I was finally getting a glimpse inside a mansion I'd long admired. Predictably, the interior was stunning, with high ceilings, ornate chandeliers, antique furniture, and everything else you'd expect from an expensive, traditionally decorated home in the French Quarter. Even the fake cobwebs, furry spiders, and other Halloween paraphernalia hanging everywhere didn't detract from the architectural splendor of the place.

Battery-operated lanterns and natural lighting through the window blinds provided the only illumination, and the air downstairs felt stagnant thanks to all the body heat and the lack of air conditioning. It made me wonder how the homeowners – or squatters – had managed to blast the music throughout the house.

Are they seriously stupid enough to waste a generator like that?

One look at the folks downstairs, who were either drinking, smoking, sleeping, or fooling around, and I had my answer.

We passed a couple making out on the stairs, and the redhead snickered but kept going. When we reached the second story, my giggling guide came to a brief halt and gazed around the stifling sitting room before proceeding through the crowd. Maybe she sought someone in particular. Or maybe she couldn't recall where she'd been headed. It wouldn't have surprised me if she'd even forgotten I was behind her.

Reluctantly, I followed her across the spacious area, which was presently packed with even more costumed partygoers than I'd seen downstairs. All in their twenties and thirties. Empty beer and liquor bottles, various pills and powders, and partially nibbled munchies lay on nearly every table, and I counted at least a half-dozen bongs being passed from person to person.

Even me – the oldest dude there – was fair game, as I discovered when a scruffy-looking guy in – you guessed it – a fucking pirate outfit offered me a hit. I looked longingly at the bong, but ultimately passed.

Throughout my life, I had smoked a bit of pot here and there: in college, while hanging out with Clare's old university buddies in Los Angeles, and during a visit to some conservative hippie friends on South Padre Island. I'd always found it a pleasant way to relax, but a few years earlier, I'd sadly discovered my middle-aged system couldn't handle the new marijuana strains.

At one of our movie nights in the courtyard, I'd taken a couple hits from a neighbor's joint, and my heart rate immediately spiked. In fact, my pulse raced faster than it ever had before. No matter what I did, I couldn't calm down, my breathing grew labored, and I thought I was going to die.

It had also freaked Clare out. Not the pot – which she, eight years younger, was still able to smoke with no complications – but my racing heart. Even slightly stoned herself, she'd followed me inside our apartment and watched me with the patience and determination of a mother hawk.

Eventually, while lying across our bed, I'd felt my heart rate and respiration normalize, and thirty minutes after taking the troublesome marijuana hits, I was fine. Just to ensure that specific strain hadn't been the problem, I tried smoking on another occasion. Got the same results.

So, my pot-smoking days were over. Besides, as much as I longed to relax with a bit of "chronic" – or, hell, an Abita beer – I needed to keep my wits, energy, and focus intact.

After declining the offer, I continued trailing the redhead across the second floor until she abruptly stopped and turned to face me. She stared at me for a moment, her eyes glassy, her brow furrowed, then walked forward again.

Yep, this chick is definitely out of it.

Still, she seemed to be in far better condition than most of her fellow revelers. Beyond the booze and pot, people were embracing an assortment of other drugs. Snorting cocaine. Popping pills like candy. Even tripping on the floor, empty syringes beside them. Excellent activities during a zombie apocalypse: They wouldn't ensure survival, but at least the partyers would feel less worry and pain while being eaten.

Frankly, I couldn't believe so many idiots had endured the night. I could only guess they'd been attending a massive Halloween bash there when the mayhem had begun. Whether they'd taken the danger seriously, it was difficult to say, but perhaps they'd merely turned the disaster into an opportunity to keep partying. Seriously, the place and the people looked like they'd already endured a weeklong celebration.

It wouldn't have been the first time that had happened, of course. Over the years, many New Orleanians and other residents of the Gulf Coast had ignored dire hurricane warnings and, instead of evacuating with their families, stayed behind to host weeklong hurricane parties, riding out the storms in style. Some figured they'd go out with a bang, while others claimed living in the present would somehow avert disaster.

Predictably, some people had perished that way, especially in historic storms like Camille and Katrina. But, as with most preventable disasters involving stupid people, such horror stories hadn't kept some locals – particularly the young ones – from stubbornly holding on to tradition.

So, their Halloween celebration had simply morphed into a zombie hurricane party, and if the morons managed to triumph, who was I to say they were wrong?

In a large bedroom, with French doors that opened onto the crowded gallery and a king-sized bed currently occupied by several entangled couples, the redhead paused again.

"Oh, yeah, I remember what I was gonna say." She stared at me for a few seconds, as if still struggling to recall her thought. Then, a wide grin lit up her face. "Can I see your cat?"

Hell, no!

I had no intention of opening Azazel's carrier in that

place.

Fuck, somebody here'll probably try to smoke her.

The girl looked so eager, though, I couldn't refuse her completely. So, following a brief warning about Azazel's unpredictable temperament, I permitted the girl to slip her hand beneath the lid atop the carrier and stroke my cat's soft fur. Usually, if a stranger invaded Azazel's space, said stranger would soon have puncture wounds on his or her hand, but that time, my ferocious tiger actually allowed the redhead to scratch her ears. Maybe she sensed the girl only posed a threat to herself.

"Her name's Azazel," I told the young woman.

"Wow," she said, "my name's Ariel." She leaned closer to the opening and gazed into Azazel's eyes. "Maybe we're related," she continued... to the cat.

"Yeah, maybe," I replied hesitantly. "Listen, I need to find a way out of this place."

"Really? But you just got here," she said as she stepped outside.

Reluctantly, I followed her onto the seriously overburdened gallery. More than a hundred people seemed to be dancing and jostling on the creaking floorboards, and as sturdy as it had always appeared from the street, the gallery now felt like a shifting boat deck.

For all I knew, it had suffered massive termite damage over the years and could no longer bear such weight and movement. Even in pristine condition, it probably wasn't rated to withstand all that pressure, and I could easily see it collapsing under the bulk of the raging party. Whatever the case, I didn't intend to stay long.

"Hey, man," a handsome, dark-haired dude dressed as a court jester said. "Welcome to my crib."

"This is your parents' house," Ariel reminded him. "Not yours."

"Well, they're probably dead now," he lamented. "So, I guess that makes it mine."

Sadly, he had a point.

The music, emanating from built-in speakers throughout the house, shifted to Dr. John's "Indian Red" – one of my favorite songs. If New Orleanians, even the young ones, had anything in common, it was their appreciation for great music. An appreciation Clare and I definitely shared.

Just as I found myself reflecting on all the wonderful local musicians and bands we'd listened to over the years, I heard a shout from the far end of the packed gallery. Apparently, one of the clueless partygoers had tumbled over the iron railing.

"Oh, fuck, man," the dark-haired jester said, pushing his way toward the railing and gazing down into the street. "Hey, Dramond! You OK, man?"

Out of morbid curiosity, I pushed forward, too, and peered over the grillwork. Good news: Dramond had fallen onto a cushion of sorts, namely the countless zombies currently crowding the building. Bad news: The poor guy had become witness to a feeding frenzy in which he was the main course. The creatures surrounding him ripped his body apart so quickly, he barely had time to scream before he died.

Only a few minutes after he fell, two zombies started fighting over his head. One had jammed its hand up his neck, while the other had stuck its fingers in Dramond's eye sockets, gripping his bloody skull like a bowling ball.

This zombie nightmare keeps getting better and better.

Just when I thought I'd seen the sickest shit imaginable... bam, two zombies began playing tug-a-war with a dude's head.

As stoned and drunk as the kids appeared to be, several of those who'd witnessed the carnage abruptly puked onto the heads of the zombies below, which only further incited the moaning creatures and made them even more eager to reach the end-of-the-world revelers. Worse, as soon as some of the guys and girls started crying, more people from inside ventured out to look down on the street. I could see the zombies pushing against the support poles below and hear the floorboards groaning loudly.

The far end of the gallery drooped, and I decided I'd stayed long enough. Quickly, I tucked my axe behind my belt, linked my right arm through those of the dark-haired boy and the redheaded girl, and yanked them back into the bedroom just as the rest of the gallery facing Royal Street collapsed, sending everyone else tumbling into the zombie-filled street below.

Chapter

16

"I think that I am familiar with the fact that you are going to ignore this particular problem until it swims up and bites you on the ass!" – Hooper, *Jaws* (1975)

The combined momentum of my two new friends caused all three of us to tumble backward onto the hardwood floor of the bedroom, knocking over a few other freaked-out partygoers in the process. Unfortunately, the inadvertent fall made me loosen my grip on the cat carrier, which rolled a couple feet away, only to be kicked back toward me by a panicked girl dressed as a sexy imp. For the third time that morning, poor Azazel ended up upside-down, and from the hissing she unleashed toward me, I knew she was pissed beyond belief.

"Sorry, girl," I grumbled as I wriggled from beneath the two stoners and reclaimed the carrier.

Although the axe tucked behind my belt had shifted in the pileup, I'd once again escaped an irreversible injury to my genitals. For that, if nothing else, I was grateful.

Rising to my feet, I surveyed the commotion. People were bolting like headless chickens in every direction, including the naked couples who'd just been having sex on the bed, and the ensuing cacophony of blues music, terrified shrieks, and hysterical crying almost overwhelmed my already compromised eardrums (thanks to a long-ago ear infection).

Carefully, I edged toward a window beside the open French doors and glanced downward onto Royal. The scene was as nightmarish as I'd expected, rife with flailing limbs, splattering brains, and blood-curdling screams. Perhaps worse, the floorboards were still hanging from the side of the house, and the poles had crumpled in such a way that the nightmare was far from over.

"Fuck," I shouted, "we have to get outta here!"

"No, man," the dark-haired jester said, shaking his

head vehemently. "We gotta help my buds."

"They're all dead," I said, looking from him to the redhead, whose tear-stained cheeks underscored her frozen stare of terror and confusion.

"Jesus, man, this is bullshit," the jester whined. "Now, I *do* hope my parents are dead, cuz if they aren't, they're gonna fucking kill me."

"Somehow, I think they'd care less about the damage... and more about the fact that you're about to die!" Clutching Azazel's carrier with one hand, I tugged Ariel from the room. "Seriously, we have to get outta here."

Numbly, the jester followed us through the madhouse until I reached a rear hallway.

Then, I turned toward the two of them. "Listen, that gallery is now a ramp."

They merely stared at me, their foreheads crinkled, their eyes squinting in confusion.

"Christ, guys, it's a fucking ramp. From the street to this floor," I explained, beyond exasperated – and confident I was about three seconds from leaving the two dumbasses in the hallway. "Soon as those goddamn zombies are done eating your friends, they're gonna climb up here and start attacking the rest of us."

Comprehension finally seemed to dawn on the jester.

When, a moment later, I heard the front doors splinter and crash into the first-level foyer, followed by a new wave of terrified screams, Ariel seemed to catch my meaning, too. The zombies were now in the house, and they'd soon be upstairs as well.

"I know a way out," the jester said as he moved toward the staircase in the spacious sitting room.

"We can't go down there," I yelled, following him to the top of the stairs. "They're already in the building."

At that moment, another long-haired dumbass took the opportunity to kneel beside me and blow pot smoke into Azazel's cage.

"Heh, heh," he chuckled. "Kitty gonna be stoned."

How the hell had the idiot missed the mayhem around him?

Maybe ignorance really is bliss.

"That is so not cool," Ariel scolded him. "You don't even know if he lets his cat smoke."

Likely meaning to push him away from Azazel's carrier, she inadvertently shoved him so hard he tumbled backward down the stairs – just as one of the invading zombies reached the lowest step. With our mouths hanging open in disbelief, the jester and I glanced at each other and then back down the stairs, where the zombie and five of his mates were devouring the screaming stoner who'd taken the fall.

The redheaded girl wore a horrified, shameful expression on her face, but the unfortunate accident had probably saved our lives. The zombies who'd converged on his body had now wedged themselves on the staircase, temporarily blocking the path from other marauding creatures.

"We have to go up," the jester said, grabbing the stunned redhead's hand and dragging her back toward the rear hallway.

Without hesitation, I followed the two of them to a narrow staircase I hadn't noticed before. Rapidly, we leapt up the wooden steps. Glancing backward, I noted several of their friends had begun to follow us. But the zombies had either cleared the main staircase or found a way up the ramp created by the collapsed gallery because, as soon as the unfortunate people reached the foot of the stairs, they were tackled from behind.

At the top of the staircase, I set Azazel's carrier on the floor and signaled for the jester to help me push a large wardrobe from the wall and pivot it onto its side to block the stairs. We managed to shove it in place just as the first undead creature reached it. With just one of them pushing against the cabinet, it held long enough for the three of us to make our next move.

I felt a tug on my elbow and turned to see Ariel pointing toward an open doorway, where the jester was waiting for me.

Quickly, I picked up the carrier and followed the two of them onto a back deck. From there, we had a hazy view of Ursulines Avenue and the zombie hordes still being lured by the music, which, sadly, no one had thought to shut off yet. I wasn't sure what my new pals had in mind, but the only exit appeared to be a multistory staircase leading to the gated driveway below.

I shut the door behind me. "Now, what?"

The jester pointed to a side gate in the wall lining the driveway. "That leads to a narrow alley behind the empty house next door. We can use it to get out – and then run like hell to Bourbon."

I shrugged. Looked like, regardless of what choice I made, I was going to die: either there in the House of Death or down in the zombie-filled streets three stories below. The worst aspect of that realization, though, wasn't so much my impending death – or even Azazel's. I shuddered instead to think of what it would mean for Clare: She'd never learn what happened to us, and without me by her side, she might not last long either.

It tore me up inside to let her down, but at the moment, I had limited options.

Might as well go down swinging.

Just as the three of us reached the driveway, we heard a crash above us and spotted at least two zombies milling about the third-floor deck. Luckily, they hadn't noticed us yet. Unfortunately, though, a lot of the screaming had faded, meaning the zombies had nearly finished brunch and would soon be searching for their next meal.

Cautiously, we opened the gate at the far end of the driveway, crept along the narrow alley behind the adjacent house, and turned onto an even narrower lane on the other side of the vacant structure. At the gate facing Ursulines, we peered through the metal bars and watched a few more zombies trickle past, en route to the pulsating buffet on the corner.

I extended my hand to the dark-haired jester. "By the way, I'm Joe."

He shook my hand and grinned. "I'm Peter." He

cocked his head toward the redhead. "That's Marci."

I turned to her. "Thought your name was Ariel?"

She smiled bashfully. "Oh, that's just my middle name." She glanced down at the carrier. "Sorry for freaking Azazel out. I've always had a thing for kitties."

I shrugged. "Hey, no harm done. I figure if you hadn't been curious about my cat, she and I would've died back there."

"Along with all our friends," Marci whispered.

"I'm sorry you had to witness that," I said. "The world turned insane overnight."

"Well, it took a little longer than that," she said, still wearing a shocked expression.

"Yeah," I replied. "Guess it's been going crazy for a while now."

"No kidding," Peter agreed. "But I'll say this, if you hadn't been there, we'd probably be dead, too."

"Yeah," Marci added. "Thanks for pulling us off the gallery in time."

For two people who'd seemed fairly stoned ten minutes before, they were both pretty damn sober now.

"Listen," I asked, "where are you two going?"

"Marci's parents have a place Uptown," Peter replied. "Think we'll try to make it up there."

"But you don't even have weapons," I noted. "Look, I'm headed to my van right now. I can take you out of the city if you want?"

Marci shook her head. "I need to see if my parents are alive. I only came over to Peter's place for the party and stayed because... well, because."

Obviously, Peter and Marci were a couple, so it made perfect sense she'd want to be with her boyfriend as the world ended. Even if they'd been too stoned to accept the reality. They'd likely figured the best way to face – or ignore – the apocalypse was to host a balls-out bash with all their pals. The ultimate hurricane party for the storm of the century – not in the hope of ignoring the typical wind, rain, and flooding outside, but a once-in-a-lifetime cyclone of the walking dead.

Hell, if I had a choice, I would've spent last night with Clare. Preferably well beyond New Orleans.

Gazing between the bars of the gate, I noted more passing zombies.

"Look," I whispered, "you two haven't been out there yet, so you don't know how it is. You're gonna be scared, and that's OK, but try not to run. Better to lumber along like they do and blend into the background. Of course, if any of them do sniff you out, be prepared to bolt as fast as you can."

They both nodded slowly.

I set down Azazel's carrier, removed my backpack, and unzipped the largest compartment. Carefully, I located two of my kitchen knives and handed them to Peter. "You both need something to protect you. These aren't much, but they're better than nothing."

"So, what do we do?" He smirked. "Go for the brain, like you see in the movies?"

I nodded. "Pretty much. Seems to be the only way to put them down for good. You hit 'em anywhere else, and they'll just keep coming for you... till they get what they want."

Marci gulped. "And what's that?"

Seriously? Haven't we been down this road already? Haven't you seen enough to answer your own question?

Grimacing, I tucked the axe in the side pouch, resecured my backpack, and picked up Azazel's carrier. "What do you think?"

She surely knew the answer but simply didn't want to vocalize it. I couldn't really blame her. I'd witnessed the zombies in action, and even I didn't want to admit the truth.

With a deep breath, I pulled the derringer from my pocket and unlocked the gate. "Remember," I said, looking at each of them, "don't run if you can help it, and whatever you do, try not to scream. That's a dead giveaway you're not one of them." I sighed. "Ready?"

They both held their knives aloft and nodded.

"Stay back for a sec. While I check to see if the coast is clear."

Again, they both nodded in compliance.

I opened the gate slowly, trying to minimize any creaking, and cautiously peeked into the hazy street. To the right, the intersection was still packed with zombies and their victims' remains, but to the left, only a few creatures meandered beside the line of parked cars. The herds had obviously converged on the smorgasbord of stoners inside and just outside the house on the corner.

Lucky for us, unlucky for them.

I turned back to my new friends and nodded, then together, we lumbered up the block toward Bourbon Street, sidestepping zombies and trying not to draw unnecessary attention to ourselves. Although I'd had my doubts about the naive couple, Peter and Marci managed to follow my instructions. Their faces reflected the fear and disgust they likely felt, but they remained calm and stalwart all the way to Bourbon.

Between the bloody Quartermaster and Myriam's quiet launderette, I paused and, after ensuring no zombies were in the vicinity, asked, "Are you sure you don't want to come with me?"

Peter nodded.

"OK, then," I whispered. "Good luck to you both. I hope you make it."

"You, too," Marci replied.

With their knives at the ready, the two of them headed northeast on Bourbon. I watched them for a moment, hoping they'd survive the day, then I continued northwest on Ursulines, past Myriam's launderette, and prayed the last three blocks of my journey would be the easiest yet.

Chapter

17

"Sometimes, the world of the living gets mixed up with the world of the dead." – Mrs. Bertha Mills, *The Others* (2001)

I covered the first block, between Bourbon and Dauphine, with little trouble. Less than two blocks from Rampart Street, however, I was forced to fire the derringer for the first time. Actually, I missed the initial shot, so I ended up using both chambers.

I'd just crossed Dauphine when a girl wearing a blood-spattered school uniform stumbled from an open alley.

Thanks to the gore, it was hard to pinpoint her age. She could've been a senior in high school, a well-developed freshman, or a twentysomething woman dressed up as a slutty parochial student. Living in New Orleans, particularly during Mardi Gras, Halloween, or pretty much any weekend, I'd always found it best not to judge.

I would've sidestepped her, as with other zombies I'd passed, but she seemed more determined than most. Once she'd gotten a whiff of me and Azazel, she had no intention of letting us go. So, as she continued toward me, I aimed the derringer, pulled the trigger... and completely fucking missed her.

On some psychological level, I could've missed on purpose: I had yet to kill a woman, and even after the bloodbath I'd just witnessed, I still found it hard to do so.

Again, I hadn't had time to think when I'd dealt with the four zombies in the courtyard. I'd merely reacted on instinct.

But, just the day before, that girl could've been hanging out with her friends or shopping for a holiday dress in one of the French Quarter's swanky clothing stores. Now, she was a fucking mindless zombie, with some asswipe pointing a gun at her head.

It was also highly probable I was simply a lousy shot.

Though I'd driven to a shooting range in Gretna, a suburb on the West Bank of the river, almost every day since receiving Samir's tell-all flash drive, I was far from a skilled sniper. In fact, I still sucked at shooting – just not as much as I had a couple weeks earlier.

In either case, chivalry or incompetence seemed like poor reasons to miss a target at less than ten feet away. So, before the once-sexy schoolgirl could get five feet from me, I pulled the trigger again, and she promptly fell to the ground, with a .38-sized hole in her forehead.

And joy of joys, the gunshots had alerted other zombies. In retrospect, I should've used the axe; compared to the derringer, it offered a much less conspicuous way to kill. I knew better than to call unnecessary attention to myself, something I'd even warned Peter and Marci not to do. But, despite my success with putting down the male half of the T-1000, I'd been worried about getting the axe stuck in another zombie skull and making myself even more of a target.

Essentially, though, pulling a trigger equated to ringing the dinner bell. From both ends of Dauphine, various buildings in the vicinity, and farther down Ursulines, toward the former party house, hundreds of zombies came trotting and stumbling toward me. Hell, I didn't wait to count them all; there could've been thousands. By the time I'd sprinted toward the next street, Burgundy, I had put some distance between myself and the hordes of zombies flowing through the Quarter.

Unfortunately, there were now half a dozen zombified creatures trudging toward me from the direction of Rampart. I slowed my pace, set Azazel's carrier onto the cab of a pickup truck, and reloaded the derringer. Two chambers made it a less-than-ideal pistol for shooting the undead. But how could I have asked Troy for a better piece when I'd felt lucky he'd given me anything at all?

As soon as I loaded the stupid gun, the six zombies had closed the remaining distance, forcing me to play some ring-around-the-rosie, Benny Hill-style bullshit just to keep the truck between me and them. Initially, they all tried to pursue me in the same direction, so I maintained a safe distance as I shot the first two in their temples. Two lucky shots that cut the number of my would-be murderers by a third.

In a rather unlucky turn of events, however, the remaining four zombies split up. Not consciously, it seemed. More like they inadvertently tripped over the corpses of their two cohorts and pinballed into one another... until one pair headed toward the hood of the truck and the other pair circled toward the tailgate. I glanced toward the intersection of Burgundy and Ursulines, realized I only had a couple minutes before the hordes had caught up with me and Azazel, and noted I had mere seconds before the four nearest zombies collided with me on the sidewalk.

Impulsively, I stepped onto the front passenger-side wheel, jumped onto the hood of the truck, and scrambled onto the cab beside my cat. From there, I aimed carefully and shot two of the nearest creatures in their foreheads: a formerly cute, bare-breasted woman painted to resemble a giant daisy and wearing about two dozen sets of Mardi Gras beads (which numerous ogling guys had surely given her before the shit had hit the fan), and a sixtysomething man dressed as an outrageous pimp.

Shooting the pretty daisy girl was no fun, even if one of her perky breasts now hung grotesquely from her sternum. The pimp, however, looked like the kind of dirty old man who'd chuckle innocently as he attempted to grab the daisy's ass: a thought that went through my head, making it much easier to put a bullet in his.

With little time to waste, I pocketed the gun, grabbed Azazel's carrier, and stepped onto the hood of the pickup truck. As I leapt to the sidewalk and bowled the two remaining zombies aside, a bit of zombie goo landed on the back of the carrier, threatening to drip between the slits.

"Don't lick that," I warned Azazel as I sprinted toward Rampart. "You'll turn into a zombie cat, and your mama will never forgive me."

I awkwardly wiped the carrier with my T-shirt – not a simple feat for an overweight guy on the run – but honestly, the smell seemed to have repulsed her anyway. Twitching her nose, she scooted toward the front gate of the carrier. She'd always been a damn smart cat, a consistent groomer, and a rather fickle eater, so I wasn't terribly surprised by her behavior. Now, if she'd been a dog, I had no doubt she'd have been lapping up that nasty shit in a heartbeat.

I rounded the corner, slowed my pace, and continued toward the familiar swinging doors of our parking lot. Although there were numerous undead creatures in both directions on Rampart, I trusted my steps were quiet enough to evade notice.

Presently out of sight of the zombies doggedly pursuing me on Ursulines, I could only hope it would take them a few minutes to figure out where their meal had gone.

Chapter

18

"You'll be sorry I ever opened the gate." – Mr. Dudley,
The Haunting (1963)

When I arrived in front of the giant swinging doors, I
made sure I was relatively alone before placing Azazel's
carrier on the sidewalk and reaching for the garage door
opener in the middle pocket of my backpack. I worried it
might've been crushed or damaged during my varied tussles
with the undead, but luckily, it appeared to be intact.

Of course, it didn't matter – since after I pressed the button, nothing happened. As expected.

The "swinging" doors couldn't swing manually – at least not from the sidewalk. They were meant to stay shut most of the time – to protect the cars, vans, trucks, and motorcycles inside from vandalism and outright theft. Tenants were only supposed to enter the lot by using the garage door opener, which, when pressed, would activate the motor attached to the doors and cause them to pivot slowly inward.

A couple minutes later – once you'd had enough time to walk or drive into the lot – the doors would automatically close. When you were ready to leave, you'd simply press the opener again.

Unfortunately, though, the power outage must've affected the whole French Quarter – if not the entire city – so the only people with electricity were those, like Troy, who'd purchased generators and gasoline in preparation for a hurricane (if not a zombie apocalypse). Without electricity powering the motor in the parking lot, the giant swinging doors weren't swinging anywhere – essentially separating me and Azazel from our much-needed transportation.

Such a situation had definitely been one of my biggest concerns regarding our inevitable trek from New Orleans.

Because, yes, the doors had malfunctioned several times in the past. Not due to an end-of-the-world event, but thanks to the asshole who owned the lot and never maintained the motor properly. In the four years I'd rented a space from him, it had crapped out over a dozen times.

As I'd done on various occasions, I would have to force my way between the old wooden doors. Luckily, after years of being pushed apart in that way, they had a little give, even for an overweight guy like me.

Being overloaded with gear and a cat, however, made it more challenging than usual. The zombie situation also made it more time-sensitive. So, after a hasty look around to ensure no unwanted visitors had edged closer, I began pushing and pulling the doors in opposite directions. Eventually, I managed to create an opening that allowed me to squeeze the carrier and my backpack across the threshold, followed by my fat ass.

Quickly, I closed the gap – to discourage any trailing zombies or looters. Leaving the lot would be more problematic, as I'd somehow have to disengage the mechanism controlling the doors and force them to open manually. I hadn't quite figured out how to do that yet, especially since the doors themselves were twelve feet high, but I hoped inspiration would strike on my way out.

I picked up Azazel's carrier and my backpack and headed into the lot. It saddened me to see so many vehicles there. Although some were stored in the lot by out-of-town residents, who frequently vacationed in New Orleans, most belonged to French Quarter inhabitants. How many of them were still alive – much less in a position to reclaim their vehicles and get the hell out of town?

Twenty steps into the parking lot, I spotted my baby: a 1988 step van that, to most people, probably would've looked like a giant, piece-of-shit delivery truck, just a little smaller than the signature brown ones used by UPS drivers. My fellow horror nuts, conversely, would see what Clare and I saw: a zombie-killing survival vehicle.

In its former life, it likely *had* been a mere delivery truck, but all that had changed when an enterprising George Romero fan – whom Clare and I had met many years before at a comic-con in downtown New Orleans – decided it would make a terrific zombie-mobile. During its impressive transformation, the guy had gone all out to craft as realistic a post-apoc vehicle as possible, with reinforced doors, steel bars across the front to serve as an effective battering ram, steel bars on the sides and across all the windows for added protection, and a red-splattered exterior painted to look as though the van had bulldozed through a herd of zombies.

Though hard to tell from the outside, my baby was also a fully equipped, self-contained recreational vehicle. It had water and sewage tanks, a bathroom with a toilet and shower, a generator, a comfy bed, the works. An ideal setup for two married adults and one ornery cat.

The owner of the van was a native New Orleanian, but by the time we met him, he'd been doing the national comic-con circuit for a while. Typically, he would drive into the exhibition hall at a particular event, encircle the van with grotesque zombie mannequins, and charge folks five bucks each to pose for a photo op. Hell, I'd even had *my* picture taken in front of it – a fact that seemed almost prophetic now.

Shortly after receiving Samir's flash drive, Clare and I had opted to unload our blue pickup truck in favor of something more ideal for living on the road during a zombie apocalypse. Having recalled the zombie-mobile from previous comic-cons, I'd phoned the guy, explained the situation, and made him an offer. Predictably, he hadn't believed my story about the imminent apocalypse but humored me anyway, as fellow Romero fans often did.

In truth, he'd been overjoyed to dump the vehicle for the five grand I'd proposed. His wife had recently given birth to their first kid, and he'd decided to trade in his comic-con business for a more stable, less travel-intensive career. Their loss, our gain – a trade he and his wife probably regretted when all the zombie chaos started.

Along with a small arsenal and a ton of other essentials, we finally had a worthy zombie-mobile, ready for the apocalypse... well, almost. It might've initially cost us five grand, but thanks to the sale of the pickup truck and Clare's ring (not to mention all the credit cards I'd never need to pay back), I'd pooled quite a bunch of money and ended up putting another seven thousand into it. With some engine repairs and a slew of alterations, the old van was now prepared for just about anything.

Admittedly, the owner of the parking lot hadn't been thrilled when I'd replaced my blue pickup with "this monstrosity," as he'd called it. Heavy and a bit unwieldy, it wasn't the easiest vehicle to park in that tight lot, and it didn't get the best gas mileage either, but in my humble opinion, the van was still a beauty. As it came into view, I finally released the overdue breath I'd inadvertently been holding. Thankfully, no one had stolen or vandalized it since the zombies invaded – a reasonable fear I'd kept from Clare.

Immediately, I moved to the front passenger side and unlocked the door. I set my backpack on the floor, placed the carrier on the seat, and buckled it in place so Azazel would be safe on the road. I closed the door and moved toward the back of the van. Since I hadn't been completely prepared to leave town, I still had a few items to stow and secure before hitting the road.

As I unlocked the door, I heard soft thuds and grunts behind me. Suspecting a zombie had found its way inside the lot, I turned to confront it and found myself staring at two young black punks atop the brick wall separating the property from the one behind it. Before I had a chance to bolt, hide, or defend myself, they had landed on the ground and aimed their handguns at me.

The tall, beefy one was likely in his early twenties, while the short, skinny one looked no older than eighteen. No doubt, their speed and stamina would rival mine – not to mention the fact that their handguns were surely loaded. Unlike my stupid derringer.

Just my goddamn luck.

Chapter

19

"You gotta be fuckin' kidding." – Palmer, *The Thing* (1982)

"Don't fuckin' move," the older one said.

I stepped toward the side of my vehicle and slowly raised my hands. "Look, guys, I don't want any trouble."

Ignoring my plea, the younger one asked, "Whatcha got in da van, man?"

I couldn't figure out the smartest way to answer his

question, so I not-so-wisely said nothing.

With his gun still pointed at me, the tall one walked toward the back door, my keys still dangling from the lock, and opened it. He pulled back a tarp I'd used to cover the weapons and gear I still needed to put away.

"Holy shit," he yelled, his gun shifting downward. "This fucker's armed to the teeth."

"Tell you what," I said, lowering my hands, "just take those guns and let me get out of here."

"Fuck no, man," the older one said, once again aiming his gun at me. "We takin' your ride."

My heart seemed to plummet into my stomach. After everything I'd been through in the past sixteen hours, I couldn't believe two thieving thugs – not ravenous zombies – were going to stop me. Even though I suspected looters and vandals could be a problem throughout the city, just as they'd been in the wake of many hurricanes, I hadn't yet witnessed any purposeful theft or destruction. Just wanton damage by the zombies and desperate acts of survival by the humans who remained.

As I stood beside the van, contemplating my options, the tall kid slid one of my shotguns from the pile. He tucked his own gun into his waistband and held out mine like a cocky sheriff from the Old West. When he took the fun too far, attempting to spin the shotgun like the Rifleman himself, he lost control of the weapon, and it clattered onto the pavement. While he scrambled to retrieve the shotgun – and his friend turned away from me to give him shit for being an idiot – I took my chance to slip toward the front of the parking space and behind the Range Rover sitting beside my van.

I knelt behind the front driver's-side tire, removed the derringer from my pants pocket, and fumbled in the other pocket for a couple bullets. With all the guns I'd stored only a few yards away, I couldn't believe I had to load the damn derringer again. How did I stand a chance against two automatic weapons and whatever else those two assholes decided to throw at me?

"Where'd you go, man?" the older one yelled. "Shit, you can't trust nobody."

"Last chance, guys," I shouted with more bravado than I felt. "Get the fuck outta here, or it's your funeral!"

"Fuck you, cocksucker," the older one replied, his voice coming from the other side of the van. "I'm gonna shoot you with your own damn gun. Gonna shoot you in the head, too, so's you don't come back as one of them dead fuckers."

"Jamal, come on, man," the younger one chimed in,

his voice getting closer to my position. "Why da hell we want dis dude's piece-of-shit van? Probably runs like crap. Let's just grab some uh dose guns an' get da fuck outta here."

Bending forward, I peered underneath the SUV. The shorter one moved between the two vehicles, edging closer to the front bumpers, while Jamal seemed to be scoping out the far side of the van. Abruptly, his shoes stopped next to the passenger-side door.

Shit. Azazel.

"What's that?" Jamal asked. "You got a fuckin' cat in here? What are you, some kind of pussy?"

The other one immediately stopped in his tracks. "Hey, man, fuck you. I gotta cat, too. Leave dis dude alone an' let's get outta here."

"Well," Jamal said, as I heard the passenger-side door open and a small hiss in response, "maybe I'll just cap the cat first."

Afraid he'd make good on his threat, I rose to my feet, stooped over in an awkward crouch, and hastened along the side of the Range Rover, toward the rear of the parking spaces. In my peripheral vision, I saw the shorter one turn toward me, but I reached the other side of the van before he could shoot me.

When Jamal spotted me, however, he immediately whirled from Azazel's carrier, raised the shotgun, and pulled the trigger.

Click.

Nothing happened, not even when he pulled the trigger again.

When he'd threatened to shoot Azazel, my paternal instincts went into overdrive – not because he had my shotgun, but because he had his own piece, and I couldn't see, from the other side of the Range Rover, which one he'd been holding. If I'd realized he was still clutching the Mossberg, I wouldn't have worried at all. Cuz the truth was... I hadn't taken the time to load the shotgun before putting it in the van.

Clearly frustrated, he tried shooting me yet again as I closed the distance between us.

"Should've used your own gun," I said as I raised the derringer level with his head.

"Fuck," he replied, likely knowing what was coming next.

With only a second of hesitation, I pulled the trigger. It wasn't a head shot, but I'd nabbed him in the neck. With a shriek, he dropped the shotgun and covered the wound, blood spurting between his fingers. I doubted he'd be any more trouble.

The other one, unfortunately, was another story. He'd dashed around the front of my vehicle before I had a chance to react. "You killed Jamal," he spluttered.

I glanced toward the ground, where Jamal writhed in pain. "He's not dead yet."

Despite my confident facade, I had mixed feelings about what had just happened. I'd always considered myself a strong man, willing to sacrifice myself for those I loved: namely, my wife, my cat, my brothers, and my parents. But while I'd always believed myself capable of killing someone who threatened me or any of my loved ones, I'd never actually shot a living person before.

Zombies, yes. People, no.

I pointed my gun at Jamal's friend – the one I hadn't shot yet – just as he aimed his gun at me. Neither of us pulled the trigger.

"What kinda gun is dat?" He crinkled his nose. "Looks old. Can't have many shots."

"It's a derringer. And two is all it needs." I sighed, knowing I had no desire to shoot the kid. "Look, my name's

Joe. What's yours?"

"Samson," he replied. "Like in da Bible."

I squinted, my eyes tracing his short stature, then arched an eyebrow.

Before I could say anything, he explained, "My mama had a strange sense uh humor."

Movement behind him caught my eye, and I realized we had visitors. Apparently, some of the zombies had heard either our voices or the gunshot and, eager to investigate the potential meal, shoved their way between the giant doors. Samson and I had run out of time.

"Seems we have company," I said.

"Zombies?" he asked without shifting his eyes – or his gun – from me.

"Listen, Samson, I don't want to shoot you, and I don't think you want to shoot me." At least I hoped he didn't.

"Naw, man," he said, glancing from me to his dying friend to the zombies heading our way. "I never wanted to do dis bullshit. Just tryin' to survive."

"Why don't you go find your mama?" I asked. "And get her outta the city?"

Sighing wearily, he nodded and lowered his gun.

I lowered my pistol as well.

"Good luck, mister."

"You too, Samson," I said, bending down to retrieve the shotgun.

I looked up in time to see him bolt past me and leap for the upper ledge of the brick wall. Some of the zombies were only a few yards away and rapidly closing on my position, so I sprinted toward the passenger door of the van and slammed it shut. As I dashed to the open rear doors, I caught a glimpse of Samson disappearing over the wall. A part of me hoped he'd make it.

Hastily, I grabbed my keys, climbed into the back of the van, shut and locked the doors, and scrambled toward the driver's seat. I'd just buckled my seatbelt and started the rumbling engine when the first zombies reached us. Ignoring me and Azazel, they made a beeline for Jamal. Probably lured by the smell of fresh blood. And his groans.

Several zombies disappeared from view as Jamal screamed. I could only assume they were tearing him apart, devouring everything in sight. His bloodcurdling shrieks were almost too much to bear.

Eh, fuck him.

He'd tried to rob me – and kill me – and ultimately gotten what he deserved.

Chuckling, I realized Robert would've been proud of my eye-for-an-eye attitude. Even if Clare would disapprove.

Carefully, I pulled out of the parking space and headed for the giant doors. The gap was much wider now, but still not wide enough for my vehicle to pass. The high volume of zombies presently flooding into the lot would make it impossible for me to stop the van, climb from the driver's seat, and manually open the doors as I'd planned.

Only one way to go.

"Sorry, baby," I whispered, before gunning the van and ramming through the doors.

The wood splintered with a deafening roar, but we made it onto Rampart Street, dismembering zombies, scraping the sides of my vehicle, and whacking the passenger-side mirror in the process. The makeshift battering ram had done its job, and the van now had real damage – and real blood – to match its fake patina.

"Oh, well," I said, glancing at the dangling side-view mirror. "Every car has to have its first scratch."

Driving northeast on Rampart, headed for the nearest I-10 entrance ramp, I could finally breathe a little easier.

True, I still had to swerve around busted cars, hapless

survivors, and zombie herds on the roadways. Hunger, thirst, and fatigue had almost derailed me a few times. My headache had returned with a vengeance. And I couldn't shake the terrible memories of being chased by zombies, seeing countless bodies in the streets, and watching dumbass stoners be ripped to shreds.

Yes, I hated leaving neighbors behind and knowing I might never again see the people and places that had made New Orleans home. And indeed, I realized more than eighty miles still lay between me and Baton Rouge.

But despite quite a few obstacles – and several close calls – Azazel and I had miraculously survived. Finally, we were headed to the highway. On our way to Clare. As we should've been hours earlier.

I patted the coin pocket of my jeans. Fortunately, I could still feel the outline of Clare's diamond ring through the denim. How futile that nearly fatal trek would've been if I'd lost the damn thing between Troy's place and the parking lot.

Glancing through the slits of the carrier, I noticed my poor cat was stretched out like a tiny manatee and snoring gently. I'd assumed that, once we reached the van, she'd start clamoring for food, treats, water, or her litter box, but she seemed beyond pooped. She'd been through a lot, too – and deserved as much peace and luck as I did.

But, since everything good in life seemed to come at a price, I couldn't help but wonder what additional horrors we'd face before making it to Clare.

Chapter

20

"The world we know is gone, but the will to live never dies. Not for us... and not for them." – Mattie Webber, *Pulse* (2006)

Naturally, getting the hell out of Dodge – or, rather, New Orleans – wouldn't be as easy as I'd hoped. Hard enough to navigate a heavy, oversized, extensively modified delivery truck – a real beast of a vehicle – around numerous dead bodies and abandoned cars (some of which were charred, smoldering, or outright burning). But the real trick to maneuvering on the narrow, pothole-filled surface streets of a post-apocalyptic Crescent City was to avoid the small – and not-so-small – herds of zombies that were seemingly everywhere.

While driving northeast on Rampart Street, I encountered a slew of undead obstacles – more than I'd observed when first squeezing my fat ass into the parking lot near Ursulines. The unavoidable gunshot that had incapacitated my would-be murderer had also lured quite a few of the walking pus-sacks from nearby buildings and adjacent side streets. Now, a bunch of mangled motherfuckers had crept across Rampart and unfortunately blocked the closest turnaround.

"What am I thinking?" I muttered to myself – and perhaps to Azazel, if she'd still been awake.

No need to wait for a proper turnaround – not today.

Abruptly, I turned the steering wheel hard to the left, and the front, all-terrain tires responded by hopping the curb and rumbling across the neutral ground – or, as the rest of the country had always called it, the *median*.

In pre-zombie days, an illegal maneuver like that would've garnered me, at best, a pricey ticket or, at worst, a painful beating by an overzealous NOPD officer. But these were different times. Since waking up in the courtyard with the axed pirate zombie, I had yet to see a living cop – just a few dead or undead ones – and traffic laws no longer existed.

In fact, all municipal laws seemed to have been suspended. Indefinitely.

Frankly, I wasn't worried about getting in trouble for driving across the neutral ground. As a creature of habit, I'd simply needed a minute to realize official turnarounds and one-way streets no longer meant anything.

No, what troubled me most about taking the unorthodox route was that, beyond typical hurdles like palm trees and streetcar tracks, the neutral ground now boasted piles of dead people. Dead, as in ravaged bodies... and dead, as in the zombies still munching on them.

The heinous scene resembled a twisted version of a traditional crawfish boil, but instead of hovering over a steaming heap of cooked crustaceans, peeling out the tails, sucking the heads, and discarding the shells onto a refuse pile, the zombies on the so-called neutral ground were pigging out on various twitching parts or fresh kills, slurping up human brains, and tossing the unwanted bones and rotting flesh aside. One seriously fucked-up feast I currently plowed my way through.

Fortunately, the zombie-mobile did its duty, shoving the ravenous diners out of our path while maintaining traction on the carnage-covered ground. I had no time – or desire – to examine the grill, tires, or undercarriage of my baby, but I assumed there was now plenty of real gore to match the comic-con paint job.

Once I'd mowed across the zombies and their unfortunate victims, and my front tires finally hit the asphalt of the westbound lanes, jolting the van and its occupants, I again turned the steering wheel to the left and headed in the right direction: what native New Orleanians would've called the "lakeside" of Rampart Street. As I passed the headquarters of the New Orleans Jazz & Heritage Foundation, I heard a plaintive meow beside me.

Glancing to my right, toward Azazel's carrier, I spotted her wide, green eyes staring at me through the slits. "Sorry, sugarplum. That was pretty bumpy, I know."

She meowed again, sadder that time.

I shifted my eyes back to the street ahead, but continued trying to soothe my little girl. "You're probably hungry. Thirsty, too. And sick of that stupid carrier. But I can't let you out just yet. For your own safety." I peeked at her again. "As soon as we're able to take a break, I promise, I'll let you roam around a bit."

She meowed once more – whether to underscore her displeasure or agree to my terms, I couldn't be sure – then she lowered her furry head and presumably went back to sleep.

Just as I returned my gaze to the road, I noticed several people darting across Rampart, probably headed to Louis Armstrong Park – a well-tended, thirty-two-acre oasis in the infamous Tremé neighborhood that bordered the French Quarter. They likely hoped the tall, iron fence surrounding the park – once a popular place for outdoor concerts and festivals – would keep them safe from the undead. I almost tagged them as I crossed St. Ann.

Gazing in my side-view mirror, I watched as the fleeing people made it mere steps from the stately front gates of the park, when a mass of zombies suddenly surged from the Quarter – surely their reason for running in the first place. Before any of the potential victims could even start to climb the gates, the undead had tackled the lot of them and, as usual, commenced ripping them into horrifying pieces.

After taking a shortcut down St. Peter and Basin

Streets, I edged closer to the I-10 entrance ramp Clare and I normally used when headed to her mom's house. It felt strange driving on traffic-free roads with nonoperational stoplights, so close to the NOPD station, St. Louis Cemetery No. 1, and other neighborhood landmarks usually bustling with people – now either overrun by zombies or hauntingly vacant.

Someone must've still been alive inside the police station because I heard several gunshots from within. Along the outside of the building, enormous piles of destroyed bodies were stacked against the entrance and near a few of the windows. The cops – or whoever was inside – certainly put up a valiant fight, but the hordes of zombies kept coming. Sooner or later, the survivors would run out of ammunition – and then they'd either starve to death, barricaded inside, or be eaten as they tried to escape.

I shrugged and kept driving.

By the time I reached the interstate entrance, I'd figured out my greatest obstacle to leaving the city. As much as I hated to admit it, Troy had been right about the highway: It was jam-packed with stalled vehicles.

Despite the suddenness of the zombie invasion, plenty of people had apparently had enough time to evacuate. Or at least attempt to evacuate. Hard to believe so many New

Orleanians had managed to reach their automobiles and hit the highway – given all the mayhem of the night before – but a strong sense of self-preservation had apparently provided the necessary dose of adrenaline and resourcefulness.

Presently, most of the cars and trucks appeared to be abandoned, with zombies weaving between both the vehicles and the bodies of those who'd unfortunately made a run for it – and ultimately lost the race. I immediately tried to bulldoze a path between the crowded lines of automobiles. With my responsive driving skills, I managed to miss most of the meandering zombies, but when a bleached-blonde woman with half of her face missing moved in front of my van too quickly, I inadvertently caught her with the front left edge of my bumper.

Although numerous obstacles made it impossible to drive fast, it was such a tight squeeze between vehicles that I simply couldn't avoid her. The van knocked her to her knees, and my bumper crushed the remainder of her face against a brand-new Lexus. Her head squished like a grape, but luckily, most of the blood and zombie goo seemed to splash onto the once-pristine hood of the luxury car. Not that I was truly concerned about how the exterior of my zombie-mobile looked.

Hampered by numerous obstacles as well as the smoky atmosphere of a city on fire, it took me almost twenty minutes just to drive a couple hundred yards. Beyond dead bodies and abandoned cars, I spotted several survivors trapped inside their vehicles, surrounded by ravenous, unrelenting zombies.

In a perverted way, the scene reminded me of those camera-wielding paparazzi encircling hapless celebrities – only the zombies wanted a bit more than a salacious photo. The undead creatures craved organs, flesh, and blood – and they wouldn't leave until they'd devoured their fill. It was a waiting game: The zombies would eventually claw their way inside or the humans would inevitably starve to death. Either way, the zombies couldn't lose.

It didn't take much longer for me to accept the interstate wouldn't work as a viable passage to Baton Rouge. Assuming I could plow my way through most obstructions, I was bound to reach a point where even the van's makeshift battering ram wouldn't suffice.

Fortunately, the I-10 wasn't my only option. Before the interstate was constructed in the 1950s, the main route between New Orleans and Baton Rouge was Airline Highway, a rather schizophrenic thoroughfare known for golf courses, schools, various businesses, and prostitutes. Lots and lots of prostitutes.

It also happened to bypass the Louis Armstrong New Orleans International Airport – hence, the name. Even if Airline were relatively empty, it would take longer than an obstacle-free interstate, but it would certainly offer more turnarounds and side streets, enabling me to avoid blockades and keep moving toward Baton Rouge.

I only hoped fifty thousand other people hadn't made the same assessment.

Chapter

21

"You want me to salute that pile of walking pus? Salute my ass!" – Captain Rhodes, *Day of the Dead* (1985)

The quickest way to exit the interstate was to put the van in reverse and retrace my route through the bodies, zombies, cars, and survivors. Out of habit, I glanced in my side-view mirror and noted a new wrinkle: At some point during my stop-and-go journey, a small BMW convertible had apparently trailed my path of destruction and now encroached upon my back end.

Seriously, who the fuck drives a soft-top convertible during a zombie apocalypse?

From what I could tell, a well-dressed, sixtysomething white man sat behind the wheel, while an attractive redhead, likely in her twenties, occupied the front passenger seat. As I rolled to a halt, shifted into reverse, and assessed my options, the jackass in the BMW honked his horn at me – possibly because he'd spotted my red taillights.

Had he learned nothing since the zombie virus had begun to spread throughout the city? Horns, gunshots, and other often avoidable sounds would only attract unwanted company.

I rolled down my window, just a crack, and yelled at him, "Hey, dumbass! Back up your stupid Beemer!"

As I'd feared, his relentless honking lured hordes of zombies from both directions. Luckily, I managed to crank up my window just as an undead clown reached his blood-smeared fingers toward the gap. Azazel and I might've been safe for now, but another look in my only functional side-view mirror told me a few of the zombies were already tearing through the cloth top of the convertible. The redhead – who was undoubtedly *not* the man's daughter – shrieked and slapped her companion's arm, probably trying to compel him to move the fucking car.

Still, despite the urgency of the situation, the entitled idiot staunchly refused to shift into reverse. Hastily, I unbuckled my seatbelt and stepped to the rear of the van, where I plucked the shotgun from beneath the tarp and loaded it with shells from a nearby drawer. When loaded, the 12-gauge shotgun could be a deadly weapon – not just a pseudo Wild West prop, like back in the parking lot.

Through the smudged windows of the rear doors, I noted three zombies clawing at the roof of the BMW. The redhead, whom I could barely see through the car's windshield, had apparently tilted her seat all the way back, so the first zombie who managed to slip his arm into the vehicle (a particularly eager postal worker) couldn't quite grab her.

Smart girl.

She might even have a chance to live if she wriggled out of the situation and away from her dumbass sugar daddy.

Not surprisingly, the driver didn't seem as quick-witted or resourceful. It appeared he hadn't thought to lower his seat, and an obese female zombie had managed to reach through the roof, grasp a bunch of his salt-and-pepper hair, and yank him upward, as if to pull her meal through the slit in the soft convertible top. The third zombie, meanwhile, had clambered onto the hood and smeared his nasty face against the windshield. I wasn't entirely sure what he was trying to do.

He's a zombie, so who the fuck knows?

Normally, I would've tried to figure out a way to avoid putting myself at risk for an ignorant stranger. But despite the durability of my van, the rear bumper hadn't been reinforced like the front – and since it wasn't a monster truck – I didn't think reversing over the BMW was an option. So, I chambered a shell and opened one of the back doors. I had to be efficient and take care of business quickly – before the zombies still lingering by my driver's-side window found their way to the open rear door.

I raised the shotgun, aimed the barrel at the zombified mailman still trying to reach the redhead, and pulled the trigger. The creature's skull exploded with the blast, leaving only its lower jaw attached to the rest of its body. As its knees buckled, its arm slipped free of the top, and the former postal worker toppled onto the concrete.

Meanwhile, I chambered another shell and swung the shotgun toward the undead fat lady still attempting to tug the driver through the roof. As I pulled the trigger, the creature moved her head just enough to avoid a kill shot. Still, the shell tore through her left shoulder, promptly separating the arm that dangled through the convertible top from her torso. Though the zombie's fingers still clutched the man's hair – a real fucked-up instance of rigor mortis – the rest of the fat lady lost her balance and stumbled backward from the vehicle.

"Put your fucking car in reverse," I shouted, noticing several more zombies headed our way. "Now!"

After that, I slammed and locked my back door. Through the glass, I watched the man fumble with something below the dashboard, presumably the gearshift, then the BMW jolted into reverse, causing the third zombie to roll from the hood onto the road.

With the zombie arm still flailing above the shredded roof, the convertible continued reversing all the way to the Orleans Avenue entrance ramp – the same one I'd used to get on the stupid interstate. Unfortunately, the two disgruntled zombies behind my van righted themselves, just as a couple additional zombies, groaning loudly, appeared from either side and banged on the reinforced doors.

My turn to get the hell outta here.

I darted back to the driver's seat, set the shotgun on the floor, and buckled my shoulder harness, then I shifted my rig into reverse and hit the gas. I felt several thumps as the van flew backward. Presumably, I'd crushed at least a couple of the zombies lingering behind my rear tires, but I didn't stop to make sure. I just kept my foot on the gas and used the driver's-side mirror to maneuver around the cars and bodies lining my path.

Regretfully, I passed some of the trapped survivors, their faces a mixture of fear and hopelessness, but there was no way I intended to stop. It was a simple mathematical dilemma: I might've had a small arsenal in my van, but only one shooter, and I'd never be able to take down all the zombies surrounding those luckless victims before getting overwhelmed myself.

Eventually, I neared my turnoff and veered backward down the oval-shaped entrance ramp – not an easy feat for an awkward zombie-mobile. When I reached the bottom of the ramp, I noticed the man had parked the BMW on

Orleans Avenue, stepped out of his vehicle, and started shaking the zombie arm loose from his head like a demented headbanger.

As I paused the van beside the BMW and considered an alternate route, the girl winked at me, slid into the driver's seat, and shifted the gearstick. Then, before the man could stop her, she tore off down Orleans Avenue. No doubt she knew what I suspected: The rich guy couldn't protect her. Not in the new undead world.

With a flabbergasted expression on his face and the stupid zombie arm still flopping above his head, he bolted down the street in his shiny loafers and struggled to chase the car on foot. Not once did the redhead stop – not even when a pack of undead ventured from a side street and hauled the moron to the asphalt.

Yep, that chick is definitely a survivor.

193

Chapter

22

"You think this is a fuckin' costume? This is a way of life." – Suicide, *The Return of the Living Dead* (1985)

After bypassing the mob of zombies feasting on the former BMW driver, I made a U-turn on Orleans Avenue and headed back toward the I-10 overpass. Now that I'd nixed the interstate as a possible route, I needed to rely on surface streets to reach Airline Highway – which meant venturing through a few neighborhoods many residents had considered sketchy and outright dangerous even *before* the walking dead had shown up.

Honestly, it had always amazed me how the city's tourism industry never seemed to take a major hit from the high crime rate. Armed robbery, assault, rape, kidnapping, and murder had all been daily threats, no matter which neighborhood New Orleanians called home. Given how compact the town was – squished between Lake Pontchartrain and the Mississippi River – none of her neighborhoods had been immune to violence and crime.

What had really surprised me, however, was how skillfully the mayor, city council, NOPD, CVB, and *Times-Picayune* staff had kept a lid on the ugly statistics – at least on a national level. A barbaric gang of thugs could rob several couples at gunpoint in the Garden District or French Quarter or Marigny, and still, the tourists and conventioneers continued to pour into the city: many because they hadn't heard about NOLA's high crime rate, and others because they simply didn't care. The Big Easy offered too many temptations to ignore.

Don't get me wrong: Despite the crime, the floods, the humidity, and the damn mosquitoes, I love New Orleans. I love her live music – the blues and the old-time jazz – and her incredible cuisine. I love the unwavering spirit of her citizens. I love her resiliency – and the way the so-called City That Care Forgot rose from the ashes of numerous fires and hurricanes and floods, a few wars, even a yellow fever epidemic. I love how she always managed to rebound from any hardship... but I guess the accurate term now would be *loved*. Past tense.

Yes, I loved the Big Easy, and I knew she'd never recover from this zombie apocalypse.

Doubt any city could.

Turning right onto North Claiborne Avenue, which ran alongside the interstate, I caught a glimpse of the vibrant murals on the concrete columns beneath the overpass. I sure would miss the art, music, movies, and books that the one-of-a-kind city had inspired during her more than three centuries of existence. There had never been any place like her – and there never would be again.

As I passed the brick walls of St. Louis Cemetery No. 2, I noticed a massive cluster of zombies in the road ahead. Afraid to press my luck against such a mob, I took a right onto Bienville Avenue and did my best to maneuver around the cars, bodies, and undead peppering the street.

Driving through the Tremé certainly differed from walking across the French Quarter. It wasn't just the architecture, but the condition of the houses that varied. Overall, French Quarter denizens had more money to maintain their structures and landscaping, so while I'd spotted a few burning buildings over there, the entire Tremé seemed to be ablaze. Sadly, the homes had lit up like kindling, the flames searing a path through the historic neighborhood.

On either side of Bienville, buildings smoldered and burned, making the air so thick with smoke that visibility became a real issue. As I crept up the avenue, wary of obstacles and lamenting the loss of an entire culture, I reflected on all the amazing experiences Clare and I had shared in the Tremé. Sampling down-home Creole food at Dooky Chase's. Catching a painted coconut at the Krewe of Zulu parade. Even watching a few second lines.

Traditionally, walking brass band parades in New Orleans were composed of two lines: the first, typically including the brass musicians and the club members who'd paid for the parading permit, and the second, consisting of those merely following the parade, relishing the music, clapping and dancing in the streets. No big surprise: During such events, second lines usually multiplied in size until they grew much larger than the original parade.

For decades, New Orleanians had used first and second lines to celebrate someone's life after he or she had died. In the Tremé, the saddest of such jazz funerals came after the shooting death of a child or teenager. Even then, though, it could be both somber and energetic – and always a memorable way for people to mourn the loss of their loved one.

Usually, the brass band would lead the mourners up and down the streets, playing traditional tunes like "In the Sweet By and By" and "When the Saints Go Marching In," luring others along the way, inspiring them to dance (and, naturally, drink) in celebration of life. Not disrespectful but, rather, expected and encouraged.

Granted, New Orleanians staged second lines to celebrate pretty much anything, from weddings to graduations. Once, I'd witnessed a dude celebrating his forty-third birthday with a second line in the French Quarter. A small brass band had led him and his plastered buddies down Bourbon Street, other people joining in the fun as they'd passed.

Only in New Orleans could you – for a few hundred bucks – buy a permit to throw yourself a parade. For no reason at all.

Sure am gonna miss that.

I'd miss seeing the Mardi Gras Indians, too. What a sight they'd been to behold.

Tough to pinpoint their exact origin. Frankly, the stories of how the tribes had formed always seemed like the stuff of myth and legend to me, but most New Orleanians had traced them back to the time when American Indians would often shield runaway slaves. The Mardi Gras Indians had become the local African-American community's way of paying tribute to such strength, sacrifice, and cultural pride.

At the time of the zombie apocalypse, the city had boasted around forty tribes, typically composed of black men and boys from the poorest neighborhoods. With names like Creole Wild West, Yellow Pocahontas, and Wild Magnolias – all mentioned in the traditional song "Indian Red" I'd just heard playing at the zombie party – those tribes were colorful and mysterious. Their members wore impressive, handmade costumes made of beads, feathers, and other vibrant materials, reminiscent of American Indian attire, and customarily matching or at least blending with the colors of each distinctive tribe.

Every tribe had various positions (like the flag boy referenced in the song "Iko Iko"), but the leader was the Big Chief. You'd have known him by his enormous feathered outfit, weighing as much as one hundred pounds (if not more), as he led his braves through the streets of New Orleans – to do "battle" with other tribes. When two different tribes would encounter each other, they would "fight" by chanting, dancing, and claiming to have the prettiest Big Chief.

It might sound weird, but it is... I mean, it was an awesome sight. I was never sure how the "warring" tribes had determined the best Big Chief. Maybe he'd simply been the loudest and the boldest – or the Chiefs had just taken turns stepping up and backing down. Regardless, though, the energy, passion, and resolve of the Mardi Gras Indians had been contagious – and a terrific way to celebrate special occasions like Mardi Gras and St. Joseph's Day.

So, it came as no surprise when I spied one last Mardi Gras Indian on my way out of town. An enormous headdress of yellow feathers framed his face, and he still clung to a yellow feathered staff. In its heyday, the outfit must've been gorgeous – and made him one proud Big Chief. But the heyday had certainly passed – for the costume and the chief.

Presently, he stumbled down the center of the two-way street, the staff gripped in one hand (perhaps out of mindless habit), his other hand dangling by mere tendons from his wrist. Nearing him, I could see long red gashes across his midsection, as though a zombie had clawed through his costume to reach the flesh beneath. He tripped into the path of my vehicle, and I caught a glimpse of his eyes – surely once dignified and defiant, now revealing the hollow glaze of the undead. And to boot, he was on fire, flames licking at the feathers, turning the vibrant yellow into charcoal.

Yep, I've got a fucking, flaming Big Bird zombie headed directly for me.

And nope, I didn't have the heart to run over him. Plus, I had no desire to collide with something on fire. So, I swung the steering wheel to the right and pulled onto someone's yard to veer around him.

I then learned my first major lesson of the day: Sentimentality had no place in the new undead world.

In my effort to avoid the blazing Big Bird, I hadn't noticed a rusted iron post in the yard. At one time, it had likely held a light of some kind, but it had since become a mere lawsuit waiting to happen. Jagged and broken, ideal for a horror-movie impaling and just high enough to clip the lower part of my radiator. As soon as I heard a thunk and a hiss, I knew I'd done some real damage.

"Fuck. Fuck. Fuck!"

Even on a cool fall day in southern Louisiana, a heavy van wouldn't last long without a working radiator. Hopping off the curb and continuing toward North Broad Street, I watched the temperature gauge steadily rise – my suspicions about the busted radiator now confirmed.

Immediately, I flipped on the vehicle's heat and cranked the blower as high as it would go. A trick that had once extended the life of an old Chevy Cavalier station wagon – by about three months.

For the first time, I was grateful Clare was elsewhere. As an adult, my poor wife had always had an extreme sensitivity to heat, and with the vents blowing full blasts of hot air, the zombie-mobile would get uncomfortable quickly. Even Azazel, who usually appreciated warmth and would willingly lie in a beam of blazing sunlight, didn't look pleased by the change in atmosphere.

"Sorry, girl," I said to the squinting eyes between the carrier slits. "Blame it on Big Bird back there."

I checked the temperature gauge. The indicator had almost reached the overheating point, the red line that says...

You're fucked – or, in this case, more than fucked. In fact, you and your cat are dead.

Luckily, the vents continued to kick out blasts of heat, which eventually stabilized the temperature. The trick wouldn't sustain itself for three months. I just needed it to work long enough for me to get the hell out of that problematic city – and on to someplace where I could repair the damn radiator.

Chapter

23

"They're after the place. They don't know why; they just remember. Remember that they want to be in here." – Peter, *Dawn of the Dead* (1978)

At North Broad, I took a left, headed southwest, and silently prayed to the gods of Detroit the van would hold out long enough for me to make it somewhere safe. I'd already endured too much bullshit to fail because of one flaming Mardi Gras Indian.

Unfortunately, I had to dodge just as many cars, bodies, and zombies on Broad as I'd encountered on Rampart. The big difference, though, was I'd noticed more of the living.

Good for them, bad for me.

The frequency of gunshots and proximity of fresh meat appeared to whip the undead into a greater frenzy than usual.

Everywhere I looked, battles were underway. From the open doors and windows of non-burning houses, people aimed their pistols and rifles into groups of ravenous zombies. I couldn't understand why the residents hadn't left town already – or at least barricaded themselves inside their homes.

I'd always respected New Orleanians for their stubborn tenacity and impressive resilience – often staying through hurricanes and other disasters to fight for what little they possessed – but without a bunch of shooters, and an even larger bunch of guns, the latest war was a losing proposition. The undead presently outnumbered the living – and were way more relentless.

Up ahead, I spotted an elderly black man, perched on

a rickety porch, pointing a shotgun into a huddle of zombies on his front lawn. I wanted to slam on the brakes and yell at him to get his ass inside, but he was too far away to understand me – and I'd only end up distracting him. Perhaps fatally.

As I neared his house, he managed to take down two of the creatures with one skillful headshot, but before he could shoot any of the others, a particularly daring predator grasped his ankle and yanked him down the steps. With a strangled cry, he vanished beneath the triumphant zombies.

So much for trying not to distract him.

A few seconds later, an old black woman bolted through the front door, hollering and brandishing a frying pan. She managed to whack a few of the zombies presumably munching on her husband, but to no avail. Inevitably, they pulled her from the porch, too.

"Fucking idiots," I hissed.

Every time someone let the zombies win, he risked becoming yet another brainless killer on the already crowded streets of my soon-to-be-former city. I felt as if I were driving through some twisted nightmare ride at Disneyland, where the animatronic critters killed and ate the tourists. What a gruesome drive as person after person got taken down and torn apart, right in front of me.

I sure hoped others who'd chosen to stay – like Robert, Myriam, and Troy – would fare better than those poor souls.

Soon afterward, I took a right onto Tulane Avenue, which would pass through Mid-City and eventually morph into Airline Highway. As I traveled from a residential area into a more industrial one, taking note of the abandoned cars, meandering zombies, and nonworking traffic lights, I had a sudden idea.

The year before, a developer had erected an enormous shopping complex on Tulane, adjacent to a relatively new outpost of The Home Depot. If I could park the van in an inconspicuous spot and safely get into the store, I might be able to find a quick fix for my busted radiator.

When I pulled into the spacious parking lot, I noticed only a handful of zombies milling about the two entrances of Home Depot. The buildings on either side of the Depot's rear access lanes were a totally different story.

On the left side, there stood a Whole Foods Market. The automatic doors appeared to be closed, but looters, zombies, or both had obviously busted out all the glass, leaving little more than metal frames and several gaping holes, large enough for undead "shoppers" to keep wandering in and out. I doubted any living people were still inside.

Was it ironic – or somehow fitting – that urban Southerners in a relatively poor area had destroyed a pricey upscale grocery and not the home improvement store next door?

Meanwhile, on the right side of Home Depot – just opposite the outdoor garden center – lay a huge Pet Mart. The rest of the complex included several small boutiques and three restaurants. I remembered when the Vietnamese place opened next to the pet store; numerous people joked its daily specials would feature dogs that hadn't been adopted the day before.

I couldn't help but wonder if any animals had been trapped inside the Pet Mart, particularly since hundreds of zombies currently surrounded the building as well as the stores and restaurants nearby. Perhaps many people would disagree, but the idea of the cats and dogs starving to death upset me more than the dead humans I'd already seen.

I knew that plenty of folks would hate me for such a sentiment, but in all fairness, most animals were completely innocent. In general, they didn't rob and rape one another as humans were wont to do.

OK, true, Clare and I had once witnessed a horrible hamster gang rape at a country hardware store outside San Diego. Perhaps thirty hamsters had dwelt in the same terrarium – apparently, a big no-no. Why? Because they couldn't handle such a living arrangement with maturity and grace. Instead, the dominant hamsters had cornered the smaller ones, making them squeal terribly – and given that all of them were males, it wasn't as though they'd been mating, but I digress...

Suffice it to say, I'd always hated to see innocent animals suffer.

Although, really, fuck those rapey hamsters.

Even after all the gross shit I'd observed, that awful scene was still seared into my brain.

I stopped the van at the far end of the parking lot to prepare my gear. Surveying my small arsenal, I opted for the Mossberg shotgun and a handy snub-nosed Smith & Wesson .38. While I'd stowed plenty of weapons in my vehicle, the .38 was the last one I'd shot at the range, so its feel was still fresh in my mind. Familiarity could help if I ended up in a tight spot.

After loading both guns, I removed the baggies of frog

powder from my shirt pocket, put some shells and spare bullets in their place, then strapped on a hip holster for the handgun. For good measure, I also stuck Troy's derringer in my front jeans pocket. Having an extra piece couldn't hurt, and unlikely as it seemed, the derringer had already saved my life several times.

Once armed, I peered out the back windows of my van and assessed the situation. The contractor entrance beneath the awning would probably work best: The glass doors appeared to be intact, and I could likely reach them without having to shoot any zombies.

Good thing, since gunshots always seem to excite the undead.

I returned to the driver's seat, put my vehicle in gear, and drove at a decent clip toward the overhang. Several meandering zombies turned at the sound of my rumbling step van, but I was more concerned about the three denim-clad creatures – perhaps former contractors – approaching the glass doors. I pressed the gas pedal to the floor and plowed right through them, only slamming on my brakes once the van was even with the doors.

One of the zombies had bounced off my bumper and

smacked into a giant concrete column. His head collided with the column first, leaving a giant red-and-black splotch behind as he fell motionless to the ground. The other two zombies were probably still twitching on the pavement, but I couldn't be sure, since I'd squashed them beneath my front tires with a sickening crunch.

Good news: I'd stopped the van so close to the doors no zombie would be able to squeeze between the gap. Bad news: I wouldn't be able to step outside until I'd pried open the store entrance.

Following my noisy arrival, I'd unfortunately attracted a few zombies toward my van. Quickly, before they reached me, I pocketed the keys, grabbed a crowbar from my toolbox, and opened the passenger-side door beside Azazel's carrier. Then, with some difficulty, I managed to jam the crowbar between the glass doors and push open one side, just enough for me to squeeze into the store entranceway.

Although I wasn't eager to leave the vehicle – and Azazel – behind, the constant heat from the open vents had made me feel lightheaded and anxious for a break. Besides, I really needed to repair the radiator, if at all possible.

Azazel looked at me through the slits of her carrier.

I touched her nose with my forefinger. "Hate to leave you, girl, but I should be right back."

Glancing through the windshield and the driver's-side window, I noticed the zombies congregating around the van. While they couldn't squeeze between my vehicle and the store entrance, they could possibly slither beneath the undercarriage, past their squished cohorts below my front wheels, and reach me, Azazel, or the store that way. So, after rubbing Azazel's furry head through the top of her carrier, I grabbed the Mossberg from the van floor, shut and locked the passenger-side door, and closed the entrance of Home Depot.

As I slid the crowbar through one of my belt loops and raised the shotgun, I found myself wishing, for the first time in my life, I was an auto mechanic – or at least the kind of guy who could've run down a Mardi Gras Indian and spared his goddamn radiator.

Chapter

24

"See. According to this, you're already dead." – Elsa, *Jacob's Ladder* (1990)

While prying open the doors to Home Depot, I'd half-expected a bunch of zombified employees in those iconic orange vests to rush me as soon as I entered the building. But, thankfully, nothing like that occurred.

Turning from the entrance, with the shotgun held high, I realized I could only see about ten yards ahead of me, where the natural light from outside spilled across the blood-stained entryway. Every time I'd visited Home Depot in the past, I'd encountered a gigantic, brightly lit, refreshingly cool warehouse, bustling with knowledgeable employees and purposeful customers.

As I took a couple tentative steps forward, though, I realized it was the darkest, stuffiest, quietest home improvement store I'd ever faced – and stupidly, I'd forgotten to grab a flashlight before leaving the van. Extreme hunger, pure exhaustion, and a constant headache made it tough to remember every necessary detail – a fact that could get me killed at some point.

Luckily, the light from the entrance windows illuminated a few nearly empty shelves off to the side, where I spotted a solitary multitool kit. I set down the shotgun, tore open the box, and discovered a drill, a circular saw, a reciprocating saw, and a pivoting flashlight, each of which could be powered by one of the two enclosed eighteen-volt batteries. Since the rechargeable batteries usually had a bit of juice, even after being in the package for a while, I attached one to the flashlight and hoped for the best.

When I flicked the switch, a strong beam of light rewarded my efforts. I retrieved my shotgun, plucked a couple plastic bags from the floor, and, holding the flashlight before me, scanned the closest aisles. It didn't take long to see the store was in shambles. Except for one bloody trail leading to the rear storage area, it wasn't the kind of gory mess indicating zombies had been everywhere, but the sort of disarray that told me looters had already ransacked the place.

Frankly, I couldn't blame the locals for hitting up Home Depot for supplies. Hell, it would've been my first choice, too. If the joint had sold food, beer, electronics, and sporting goods, I might've never gone anywhere else.

Once I'd stepped over and around the debris and reached the small automotive section, the truth became apparent: I probably wouldn't find any useful tools or supplies to mend the radiator. Pretty much everything of value or relevance was gone.

I did, however, grab a bottle of hand sanitizer and a few tree-shaped, pine-scented air fresheners. Since I was covered in zombie gore, I assumed the van smelled awful – and it would only get worse if I had to blast the heat for a while. Obviously, I'd gone nose-blind to my vehicle's interior, my sense of smell having adjusted to the foulness, but I didn't want Clare to have to deal with that odor all the way up to northern Michigan. No doubt she and her mom had already endured enough.

I moved toward the aisle normally featuring countless varieties of tape, from packaging to electrical to duct, but looters had gutted that section, too. On one of my previous supply runs, I'd purchased several packages of Gorilla tape to store in the van, but I'd accidentally left all the rolls at the store.

A self-reliant curmudgeon at heart, I'd long been a fan of self-checkout lanes. They did, however, have one major drawback: nobody to blame but myself for scanning the tape, shifting it over to make room for more merchandise in the bagging area, and then forgetting to put that particular bag in the cart before leaving the store.

"Shit. Shit. Shit."

Even though I'd mumbled the words, my voice echoed eerily in the dark, silent store. I certainly hoped I was alone because, otherwise, I'd likely just attracted some walking corpses. After a moment of listening for any telltale rustling or groaning sounds, I still couldn't hear anything but my own breath and the blood pounding in my ears.

While I hadn't had much luck yet in finding any

helpful supplies, I decided to continue combing through the store. Figured I might as well look around, just in case I spotted some tool or material I could use to repair the hole in the radiator.

By the time I reached the far side of the store, I no longer needed the flashlight. The sliding doors leading into the outdoor garden center were ajar, and plenty of natural light spilled across the threshold. As with every other branch of Home Depot I'd encountered, a fifteen-foot-high, chain-link fence surrounded the garden center, so unless someone had breached it in a spot I couldn't see, it seemed like the place was secure.

Standing on one side of the open doorway, I shoved the flashlight into a plastic bag hanging from my wrist, held out the shotgun, and poked my head into the garden center. Although looters had obviously picked through that section, too, I still observed rows of potted plants, stacks of soil, and racks of various gardening tools – items apparently less tempting in a crisis. The metal roof of the building extended over the space, a few feet above the fence, creating a pleasant outdoor area, protected from the city's frequent rainstorms.

To be honest, if you had some food and water, Home Depot wasn't a bad spot to wait out the zombie apocalypse. True, looters had depleted some of its resources, but it still housed a slew of useful supplies, including a shitload of generators and propane tanks, which could run necessary items like lights, grills, fans, and heaters for quite a while.

It also had fewer entryways to barricade than a typical shopping mall. In addition, that particular branch was close enough to the adjacent strip mall that, with a makeshift roof-to-roof bridge, survivors could easily access the nearby restaurants and their food stores, especially any nonperishable items.

Naturally, I had no intention of camping at Home Depot. I needed to get back to Azazel – and find a way to reach Clare. Still, I couldn't help but wonder how someone might fortify the place.

As I shook off my curiosity and tried to formulate a new plan for fixing my van, I noticed a fiberglass extension ladder dangling from a thick rope. Tracing the rope, I realized someone had snaked it through two of the roof supports and attached it to an ultra-expensive ATV parked near the open entranceway. Seemed as if previous looters had also considered creating a bridge to reach the adjacent shopping complex – and perhaps someone had interrupted their project midstream.

Despite my hunger, thirst, and fatigue, I was still full

of adrenaline from fighting off and running from zombies all day – and alert enough to feel my "spider-sense" tingling. Instinctively, I ducked my head just as a sledgehammer swished past my peripheral vision and smashed into the door frame beside me. My momentum caused me to tumble forward into the garden center, crashing into a planter containing a thorny rose bush and losing my shotgun, crowbar, flashlight, and extra ammo in the process.

"What the fuck?!"

My inadvertent outburst attracted the notice of some of the zombies between buildings. Their heads turned toward the garden center, their groans loudened, and a few of the more eager creatures shook the chain-link fence. It wasn't my smartest moment, but I didn't care. The thorns from the rose bush had penetrated my jeans and punctured my thighs, shooting bolts of pain throughout my legs.

Still, I didn't have time to focus on my latest injury. From the sound of footsteps behind me, I sensed the person who'd swung the sledgehammer had followed me into the garden center. Quickly, I rolled away from the thorns and onto my back, pulled the .38 from my hip holster, and aimed it toward the entranceway.

"No, don't shoot," a young female voice cried from the shadows to my right.

Glancing from side to side, I couldn't see the owner of the voice – or my assailant.

"Pawpaw," the unseen woman said, "he's not a zombie."

Suddenly, the scene came into focus, and I realized a wizened eighty-year-old man, wearing khaki pants and a long-sleeved Oxford shirt, stood just inside the garden center, the sledgehammer raised above his head, ready for another swing. His slender arms trembled as he tried to keep the weapon aloft, but the determination in his eyes made it clear that, though not an easy feat for him, he would do what he could to protect himself and his loved ones from the walking dead.

"I'm not a zombie," I assured him, aiming my pistol toward the pavement.

Slowly, the elderly man lowered the sledgehammer, his eyes still squinting with suspicion. "You're not?"

The smart ass in me wanted to remind him I was armed and having a conversation with him – not typical practices of the undead – but at the last second, I thought better of it and simply shook my head.

"Well, son, you don't look too good," he said, resting the head of the sledgehammer on the ground.

"Yeah, you really don't," the unseen woman agreed.

"Are you alright?"

The old man shifted his eyes from me to the shelves beside him. I followed his gaze to a slim, dark-haired woman in her early thirties, sporting denim overalls, sandals, and a lopsided ponytail. Nimbly, she climbed down from an upper shelf, where she'd likely been hiding since my unexpected arrival.

Movement in my peripheral vision made me look back at the old man. An older woman, about his age, stepped from behind him. Dressed in woven loafers and a denim dress, she wore her gray hair in a tidy bob, carried an old-fashioned pocketbook, and seemed altogether less rumpled than the old man and the young woman. As she scanned my gore-covered clothes, her eyes widened, and a small shriek escaped her lips.

Chuckling, the old man released the sledgehammer, stepped forward, and extended his hand, as if to help me up. "Sorry I scared you, but you would've tried to kill you, too, if you'd been me."

Letting him tug me to my feet, I was surprised by his strength. "The shotgun didn't give you pause?" I asked, leaning down to collect my fallen weapon, tools, and ammo.

He laughed sheepishly. "I admit, my eyesight ain't what it used to be. We heard the truck outside, and knew someone had opened the doors, but the way you were creeping around in there, we couldn't take any chances."

"Besides," the old woman added, "have you seen yourself? You're a bloody mess."

"Yeah," the young woman agreed, waving a hand in front of her nose, "and you don't smell too great either."

Now, it was my turn to chuckle. "Not surprised to hear that." I held up the plastic bag still hanging from my wrist. "That's why I grabbed some sanitizer and a few air fresheners for the road."

"Maybe you should just change your clothes," the young woman suggested. "Or better yet, burn them."

"Not a bad idea. That'll be next on my to-do list. After fixing my radiator. And my mirror."

The old man laughed again. "Well, now that we've cleared that up... I'm Alvin Summers." Pointing to the old woman, he said, "This here's my wife, Ellen."

She smiled at me, and I nodded in return.

"That young lady," Alvin continued, thumbing toward the dark-haired woman, "is my granddaughter, Jenny."

"Nice to meet you all." I almost added how refreshing it was to encounter people not dressed in Halloween costumes or skimpy lingerie, but I managed to keep my snarky side in check. For once. "My name's Joseph Daniels. But most folks call me Joe." I nodded toward the dangling ladder. "So, what's happening here? Looks like I interrupted some kind of grand plan."

Chapter

25

"It's nice to see that you've all bonded through this disaster." – Steve, *Dawn of the Dead* (2004)

In a lucky turn of events, the four of us had one major trait in common: We all loved non-human animals, to the point where we preferred most of them to people. Although none of the Summers trio currently had any pets, Alvin and Ellen regularly cared for the feral cats around their Bywater home, while Jenny enjoyed walking the neighbors' dogs in her Uptown neighborhood.

Once we'd moved our conversation into the main building (away from the aroused zombies), it didn't surprise me to learn the three of them had been volunteering their time for a pet adoption event in the nearby Pet Mart when the proverbial shit had hit the fan.

"We were helping the local chapter of the Humane Society," Jenny explained. "To find forever homes for a bunch of rescued cats and dogs."

Not a bad way to spend Halloween. Certainly more charitable than pursuing the holiday's typical debaucherous activities. I almost said as much, but didn't want to interrupt Jenny's tale.

Apparently, while on an afternoon break, she and her grandmother had followed Alvin to Home Depot, where he needed to pick up a few gardening tools. Soon afterward, a mangled adolescent had wandered into the store, torn a chunk of flesh from an employee's wrist, and jump-started total chaos. Once the employee had died, inexplicably returned as a zombie, and bit a concerned manager, the rest of the staff had decided not to take any chances.

Fortunately, Home Depot had had plenty of staff members and potential weapons, so with the Summers family and a few other customers lending a hand, they'd donned some waterproof rain ponchos and handily exterminated any zombies wandering through the automatic doors. As Jenny recounted the early hours of the zombie apocalypse, I silently applauded her and her cohorts' resourcefulness: If I had thought to wear a poncho, I could've spared at least two sets of clothes.

As expected, some of the customers and staff members had disliked the idea of murdering infected humans. Hard as zombies were to fathom, though, seeing had definitely led to believing – at least for most of those present.

Once the waves of undead had subsided enough to secure all the exits, the survivors had tried to ignore the sounds of terror in the parking lot and the surrounding buildings and waited for help to arrive. When that didn't seem likely, the remaining customers and employees had made a run for their cars, determined to check on their homes and loved ones. Some had reached their vehicles, some hadn't, but eventually, only the Summers family remained.

"We've been trapped here ever since," Ellen lamented.

"Yeah," Jenny confirmed. "Plus, once our phones died, and the local stations stopped coming through on the TV and radio in the break room, we weren't sure what was happening in the rest of the city."

"But we figured it wasn't good," Ellen added.

"So, we've done our best to make this place home," Alvin said. "Moved those unfortunate souls to the back, by the loading dock. Took advantage of the food in the break room. The couches, too."

"And when the looters started coming," Jenny added, "we just hid and watched and waited for them to leave. Knowing they'd break the glass to get inside, we kept the doors unlocked. So, until the power went out, they just opened and closed automatically. And luckily, everyone who came here seemed more interested in stealing supplies than destroying the joint."

I nodded. "Home Depot's not a bad place to hunker down for a while. I was thinking the same thing when you tried to hit me with a sledgehammer." I glanced at Alvin, who shrugged sheepishly. "But why didn't you all make a run for it, too? I mean, you can't stay here forever."

"Maybe not," Jenny conceded. "But we can't leave the animals behind either."

As it turned out, the three of them desperately wanted to rescue the remaining animals from Pet Mart. Sadly, they realized all those who had already been adopted during the Humane Society event were probably dead, but they hoped to save the rest if possible.

"If this really is the end of the world," Ellen said, "then the least we can do is make sure the animals are safe. Even if it's just for a little while."

"That's why we were trying to lift the extension ladder," Alvin explained. "To bridge the gap between stores."

"Only trouble is... I'm scared of heights," Jenny confessed. "And Pawpaw, strong as he is, can't do it alone."

Son of a bitch.

The big-hearted Summers trio certainly understood which buttons of mine to push. I might've created a blog to help a few people deal with the imminent zombie apocalypse – and to atone for a lifetime of selfishness – but in reality, I didn't mind being selfish. I loved my wife, my kitty, my brothers, and my parents. As for the rest of humanity... *meh.* True, I had a few friends I genuinely cared about, but in general, I'd always despised most people.

Other animals, as I've said, were an entirely different story. Don't get me wrong: I could never go vegan. Figured eating chicken, pork, beef, and seafood was all part of nature's circle of life. *Hakuna matata*-type shit. OK, I might've mixed up my *Lion King* references – I was always a bigger fan of Kimba the White Lion anyway – but my point was still accurate. Despite being an omnivore, I had always loved non-human animals.

During college, I'd spent one summer as a nighttime security guard for a small zoo near the Michigan State campus, and every night, I would hang out with the animals. Well, that might've been a stretch. I didn't enter any of the enclosures – I wasn't totally insane – but I definitely interacted with them. I'd race alongside the wolf and lion exhibits, urging the mighty beasts to chase me back and forth. They never snarled or growled at me. Perhaps one or two of them had longed to eat me, but I'd like to believe they knew I was their friend.

Of course, my pride and joy was Sharie, an African elephant who'd previously been in the circus. After being rescued and brought to the zoo, she'd never gotten along with the other elephants. I'd told her they were just jealous because she could dance – which she really could – and no matter what, she would always be my girl.

Every night I was on duty, I'd punch my timecard and start patrolling, and every night, Sharie would be waiting for me. Once she'd performed her dance, we'd play toss with an empty, two-liter Diet Coke bottle – sometimes for what seemed like hours. Although I'd visited with all the animals at least once each night, I'd mostly hung out with Sharie.

So, it had understandably saddened me when the staff abruptly transferred her to a zoo in Kentucky, where she would live among other circus-trained elephants with whom she might be more comfortable. I'd wanted her to be happy, but still, I missed her, and it hurt that I hadn't even had the chance to say goodbye.

Since then, I'd been the daddy of two rescue kitties (the first of whom had died a couple years before we adopted Azazel). If I could've afforded it – or my current cat had allowed it – I would've cared for a lot more than that. Consequently, Jenny didn't need to ask me twice to help her and her grandparents rescue the animals from Pet Mart. Still, we needed to accomplish the mission quickly. I wanted to be back on my way to Clare as soon as possible.

Once the zombies had ambled away from the fence surrounding the garden center, I'd merely needed to stand outside and listen to the mournful meows and barks underscoring the moans and groans of the undead that surrounded the pet store – and I was a goner. A dog howled, and I sighed. Jenny and her grandparents probably knew an easy mark when they saw one.

After checking on my vehicle – to ensure no zombies had breached it and gone for Azazel – I helped the Summers family gather some clamps, bungee cords, and sheets of plywood. Then, Alvin and I climbed up the fifteen-foot fence, carefully straddled the top bar, and laboriously extended the fiberglass ladder to the rooftop across the access road. It was so heavy and awkward we almost dropped it a few times, but eventually we were able to clamp the ladder to the metal roof of Home Depot.

Via a set of stairs in the rear storage area – which, sadly, looters had also picked clean – we accessed the roof and cautiously secured the ladder to the other rooftop. Not an easy task, especially given the curious zombies below, but with patience and by taking turns (for weight considerations), we were able to stabilize the ladder on both ends and tie down the pieces of plywood to it as well. In the end, we'd created a relatively sturdy bridge that would allow us to move safely between buildings.

"OK," I said, once the four of us had congregated in the break room for some much-needed water and snacks, "the first thing we need to do is get into Pet Mart and get rid of any zombies that might be inside."

When I'd initially driven into the parking lot and surveyed the scene, I'd assumed the front doors of Pet Mart were closed, but that didn't guarantee the store was devoid of the undead. Luckily, the cats and dogs up for adoption had been resting in locked crates, so even if zombies had invaded the store, the animals were likely safe. I'd yet to see a zombie turn a doorknob, let alone undo a latch and open a cage.

Then again, hunger and determination could be huge motivating factors, especially for the undead.

"Once we secure the store and rescue the animals," I continued, "I can take you all somewhere safe."

Shaking his head slowly, Alvin grasped his wife and granddaughter's hands atop the table in the break room. "We've talked it over, and we've decided to stay. Now that you've helped us with the bridge, we can make this home for a while."

"No doubt you'll find enough food, water, and other supplies to keep you going, but still... You sure?"

Ellen's face lit up with a warm smile. "We're sure. But thanks for the offer."

"What about you?" Jenny asked, her smile as friendly as her grandmother's. "You're welcome to stay with us."

"I appreciate the invitation, but after we take care of the animals, I need to push on. Can't keep my wife waiting much longer."

For just an instant, I saw Ellen and Jenny exchange a furtive glance, perhaps implying what they really thought of my plan – and the slim possibility I'd ever find Clare alive. But I couldn't afford to think that way, especially since I had to keep my head straight for what I needed to do at the pet store.

While I'd only known the Summers clan a short time,

I hated the idea of leaving the three of them behind. To be honest, though, they'd opted for the same plan I'd considered: to secure the buildings in the shopping complex, rely on the supplies in the varied stores and restaurants, and stay at Home Depot as long as they safely could. If my wife hadn't left the city – and I didn't firmly believe I'd see her again – I might've stayed, too.

Chapter

26

"I think the dead should shut up, unless there's something to say." – Patient X, *The Exorcist III* (1990)

Though willing to assist the Summers family with such a noble (if insane) task, I didn't really fancy venturing into the Pet Mart by myself. I had no idea how many zombies were inside, and given how dark the store likely was, I could easily imagine my solitary rescue mission heading south rapidly. But who should I wrangle into coming with me? How fleet-footed and gun-savvy could Alvin and Ellen possibly be? And as for their granddaughter...

"So, Joe, what's the plan?" Jenny asked, interrupting my train of thought.

"I'm still working on it, but I think it'll involve entering the store through the roof... and trying not to get myself killed."

"Don't worry. I'll have your back."

"What?"

She grinned. "I'm going with you."

While part of me breathed a sigh of relief, the rest of me faced a whole new set of concerns. "I appreciate the help, Jenny, but, uh... how should I put this? Aren't you afraid of heights?"

"Well, 'afraid' might be overstating it. I just get nervous, that's all."

"You do realize we have to cross a narrow plank bridge nearly twenty feet above the ground, with a bunch of brain-eating zombies down below, hoping we'll fall?"

She swallowed involuntarily, but before she could respond, her grandfather expressed his own displeasure.

"You're not going anywhere, young lady. I'll help Joe

with the animals."

"Don't be ridiculous," she snapped. "You need to stay behind and protect Mawmaw. Besides, I'm much faster than you."

"I agree with Al," Ellen interjected. "Let the men handle this one."

"Darn it, Mawmaw. This isn't 1950. I am perfectly capable of doing anything a man can do."

Well, not everything.

Of course, I didn't plan on jumping into their family discussion. Just stayed out of it and waited for the three of them to reach a decision.

The volley of points and counterpoints continued for a minute or so, until Alvin and Ellen finally agreed to let their granddaughter – admittedly, a mature woman of thirty – accompany me to the pet store.

Thus far, the Summers clan had survived without guns, but it felt wrong to leave the old couple unarmed – and I definitely couldn't let Jenny enter a potential den of zombies without a decent weapon. So, I returned to the contractor entrance, cautiously pried open the glass doors, and surveyed the area beneath the awning. Thanks to my earlier outburst in the garden center and the noisy task of building the bridge, all but a couple zombies had migrated to the access road between buildings.

Slowly, I unlocked and slid open the passenger-side door, climbed into the van, and crept toward my arsenal. For Jenny, I chose a fairly light 9mm Beretta with a twelve-round ammo clip, hopefully more than sufficient for our ill-advised venture. For Alvin, I grabbed another shotgun and a handful of shells.

On my way toward the open door, I heard a mournful meow. Gazing downward, I noticed Azazel staring at me through the slits of her carrier. My poor cat had been cooped up all day. She would surely need to hit the litter box and get some grub once we got back on the road.

After glancing through the windshield and the rear windows, I realized the closest zombies had yet to notice me moving through the van. So, I took a break to stroke Azazel's furry head, toss a handful of kitty treats into her carrier, and pour a little water into the small trough attached to the gate.

While she likely wouldn't have minded a chance to stretch her limbs, I didn't have time to oversee her explorations, and there was no way I'd let her roam around the van on her own. Knowing her, I figured she'd end up lying on the dashboard, grooming her fur, and attracting every zombie in the parking lot.

"I realize this stop is taking a little longer than

planned," I whispered to her, "but I promise we'll hit the road soon."

Quietly, I shut and locked the van door, sealed the store entrance, and returned to the Summers clan, who waited for me at the bottom of the roof access stairs.

"Sorry to make you all wait. I had to take care of my cat."

Obviously, the animal-loving family understood.

After handing Alvin the extra shotgun, the derringer, and some ammo, I led him and the two ladies to the roof of Home Depot. There, Ellen squeezed Jenny so tightly that even I started worrying we wouldn't return from our trip to the pet store.

Alvin, meanwhile, shook my hand. "Good luck, Joe. Take care of our girl, OK?"

"Will do."

The initial hurdle, of course, was crossing the plank bridge. The fiberglass ladder we'd used as the base could extend to twenty-four feet and hold up to three hundred pounds – not enough for both of us to traverse safely – so I volunteered to go first.

While I'd always been more afraid of water – specifically, drowning – than heights, I didn't trust our building skills or my natural balance enough to walk across the bridge. Instead, I opted for the less manly approach of crawling over the plywood.

With the .38 secured in my hip holster, the crowbar awkwardly tucked inside my jeans, the shotgun gripped in my right hand, and a plastic bag containing the flashlight dangling from my left wrist, I ventured across the fifteen-foot gap between buildings. Every creak or shift of the bridge caused me to hold my breath, especially since thirty or more zombies waited hungrily below, moaning loudly and monitoring my slow progress like scavenging vultures circling their dying prey.

Not dead yet, fellas.

I wanted to yell at them. But I kept my mouth shut, convinced one arrogant move would cause me to slip and prove them right.

When I reached the roof of the Pet Mart, I scrambled to my feet and turned to cheer on Jenny. She was already kneeling on the far end of the bridge, a machete gripped in one hand and the 9mm clutched in the other, but based on her wide eyes, ashen face, and trembling pout, I knew she was terrified – and undoubtedly questioning her promise to go with me. True, the gap between buildings was only about fifteen feet wide, but the twenty-foot drop into a pit of zombies would give anyone pause, particularly someone who was afraid of heights.

"It's OK, Jenny," I said. "I can handle it on my own." Not that I wanted to. Even Clare, who also loved animals and understood my ongoing desire to save as many as possible, would've balked at the crazy-ass stunt.

"No, no," she said, her voice wavering. "I can do this."

"Just take your time. There's no rush."

Although I'd hoped to reach Baton Rouge before nightfall, I knew what I wanted didn't matter. I only had a few hours of daylight left – and given my radiator dilemma and the obstacles I was likely to encounter, it would surely take me longer to get there anyway.

"And keep your eyes on me," I advised. "No need to look down."

With a fortifying breath, Jenny started her journey across the makeshift bridge. While she crawled at a sloth's pace, she managed to ignore the groaning zombies huddled below (and stretching their arms toward her) until the halfway mark. That was when she inadvertently looked downward, noting the ravenous creatures, and her progress came to a screeching halt.

Even with me, Alvin, and Ellen offering supportive words, we couldn't break through her sudden catatonia. Frozen in place, on her hands and knees, she simply stared at the zombies and started to hyperventilate.

I crouched toward the ground, my old soccer-playing knees popping every inch of the way. Keeping my face level with hers, I softly whispered her name. "Jenny... Jenny, listen to me. You can totally do this. You're already halfway across. Just keep your eyes on mine and take it one step at a time."

When she failed to move or even make a sound, I decided to try a new approach.

"Jenny," I shouted. "Listen to me, goddammit. If you don't snap out of it and cross this fucking bridge, I'm leaving your ass here. I'm risking my life to help you and your grandparents, but I can't stay here forever. My wife needs me." I stopped to take a breath. "And besides, I thought you said you could do anything a man can do. If that's true, prove it."

Still standing on the opposite roof, Alvin and Ellen both wore horrified expressions, but as guilty as I felt for yelling at their granddaughter, the "tough love" tactic seemed to work. Gradually, Jenny lifted her head and steadied her breathing. Then, with her eyes fixed on mine, she advanced across the bridge.

True, her pace was excruciatingly slow: She would slide her gun-wielding right hand forward a few inches, followed by her right knee, then push her machete-gripping left hand forward a few inches, followed by her left knee, then repeat the whole process. As I watched her, the tension in my chest increased until I thought I might begin hyperventilating, too.

Eventually, though, she reached the Pet Mart roof. Alvin, Ellen, and I all seemed to exhale with relief as she rose to her feet.

I smiled at her reassuringly. "I knew you could do it." As a married man, I was no stranger to the necessity of white lies.

"Well, that makes one of us," she confessed, her cheeks blushing with shame. "I had a full-on panic attack out there. How the hell am I supposed to get back to the other side?"

I chuckled. "Why don't we cross that bridge when we get to it?"

She grinned in spite of her fear and embarrassment. Then, after giving her a few minutes to calm down, I led her to the access door I'd already discovered while constructing the bridge.

Normally, I would've preferred using quieter weapons like the machete and crowbar for such a zombie-killing mission, but we'd already decided well-aimed gunshots would be more efficient. With any luck, the sounds would also lure the zombies away from the bridge and toward the front of the pet store.

Once Jenny had clipped the machete to her overalls and readied the flashlight and handgun, I pried open the door, tucked the crowbar behind my belt, and ventured inside the darkened Pet Mart. Although I assumed the stairwell led to a second level, not the ground floor, I couldn't be certain who – or what – we would soon encounter. I just hoped the animals – whose mournful meows and barks echoed from below – would endure a little longer. Or else, Jenny and I would be tempting fate for no reason at all.

Chapter

27

"Fight now, cry later." – Seth Gecko, *From Dusk Till Dawn* (1996)

Because the roof access door had been locked, as expected – and I'd had to pry it open with my crowbar – the animals weren't the only ones making a ruckus. The scraping and thudding from our unavoidably noisy entrance had incensed the undead as well. We could hear quite a bit of groaning and moaning as we descended the stairs.

"Sounds like more than a few zombies," Jenny

lamented from behind me, the flashlight beam jiggling as she navigated the steps.

"Yeah, I'm hoping it only seems that way," I replied, aiming the shotgun directly ahead. "Even a handful of voices can sound like a lot in a large space."

Not that I really believe that crap, given my luck.

We emerged cautiously from the stairwell, stepping onto a second-level catwalk that ran alongside a row of open offices, at the rear of the building. As predicted, the store's interior was rather dim, but between the flashlight still clutched in Jenny's hand and the natural light spilling through the office windows and front glass doors, it was bright enough for us to navigate along the catwalk. Good thing, too, as we apparently had to cross the entire width of the building to reach the staircase leading to the ground level.

The power outage hadn't only made it tougher to see. Without the air conditioning required to cool the enormous store, Pet Mart was also stuffier and smellier than I would've preferred. Though I caught a whiff of animal feces and funkiness, it was, of course, the smell of blood and rotting flesh that threatened to overwhelm me and Jenny. But we had a job to do, and the sooner we did it, the sooner I'd be on my not-so-merry way.

Just a few paces along the catwalk, we spotted our first zombie. He'd just emerged from one of the far offices and, unfortunately, spotted us as well. He was an older man, perhaps in his late fifties, with a shredded, gore-splattered Oxford shirt, a rotund belly full of gaping wounds, and a bushy beard matted with blood.

"Oh, my God," Jenny whispered from behind me, the flashlight beam wavering across the creature. "That's Mr. Jones. The manager."

It didn't matter what he used to be.

Right now, he's just a big ol' mess stumbling down the catwalk, headed directly for us.

From the trembling sound of Jenny's voice, I knew she didn't share my opinion. A quick glance at her stricken face, her watery eyes, and I realized she wouldn't be able to shoot someone she'd once known as a human. In her defense, I hadn't had to pass that particular test yet either.

"Cover your ears," I told her.

Nodding sadly, she pressed the flashlight against one ear and the pistol against the other. I faced forward again and aimed my shotgun. Now, it was just Mr. Jones and me, and neither of us would be smiling.

Back in the van, I'd decided to load the Mossberg with buckshot and slugs, assuming both would prove to be useful. Planning to alternate between the two, I'd loaded the buckshot shell first. Keeping the shotgun trained on the former manager, I watched and waited as he tried to close the gap between us. When he was only ten feet away, Jenny gasped from behind me – likely surprised I'd allowed him to get so close. I promptly squeezed the trigger and put a dozen holes into the zombie.

One of the shots must've severed his spine, as he immediately collapsed onto the catwalk, about five feet from us. Although he'd lost the ability to ramble, he wasn't done yet. As soon as he hit the floor, he began pulling himself across the metal grates toward us.

At that moment, Jenny's moist eyes became full-on waterworks. Doing my best to ignore her amplified sobs, I aimed the shotgun downward and put a slug through the zombie's skull. The exploding head didn't do much to stop her crying – and now, I had even more gore on my sneakers.

Even worse, the commotion had alerted perhaps half a dozen other zombies in the store. From our vantage point above the sales floor, we could see them moving through the aisles, edging closer to the catwalk.

I turned to Jenny, who was gazing over the railing and weeping even harder now.

She pointed the flashlight toward two zombies – a bloody male and an even bloodier female – near a bin of furry pet toys. "That's Tim and Sharon," she informed me between sobs. "They work with us at the Humane Society."

Damn it.

Another two creatures she wouldn't be able to shoot.

"OK," I said. "New plan. You stay up here and tell me where the zombies are." I nodded toward the so-called Tim and Sharon. "I'll go down and take care of those two first."

She sniffed, then nodded, suddenly looking much younger and more helpless than her feisty, thirty-year-old self.

Fucking fantastic.

Basically, I was on my own, which is exactly what I

didn't want. I'd never planned on getting involved with other people's problems. Just aimed to reach Clare any way I could. And yet, there I was, venturing down into a pit of flesh-eaters like some zombie-killing expert.

What a bunch of bullshit.

Chapter

28

"Come and get it, you undead sack of shit." – Elvis Presley, *Bubba Ho-Tep* (2002)

After loading my shotgun with a couple more slugs and checking the six cylinders of my .38 revolver, I left Jenny behind. As I crept past the open doors on my left, I glanced into each office, ensuring no more zombie surprises awaited me. Once I reached the far end of the catwalk, I realized Mr.

Jones had been the only active zombie on the second level.

Unfortunately, though, he hadn't been the only victim. In each of the five offices, I'd spotted at least one bloody mess of a brain-dead corpse, and on the catwalk itself, I'd had to step over several random body parts.

What a fucking horror show.

Standing at the top of the metal staircase, I aimed my .38 at Tim's head as he reached the lowest step. Given the angle, the distance, and the wavering flashlight beam, it took four shots to put him down.

Shit. Shit. Shit!

Sharon attempted to step over her former partner's body, presumably to reach me, but thanks to her clumsy gait and lack of coordination, she ended up getting her right foot caught in Tim's torso. Even from my vantage point, I could see a gaping wound where his stomach had once been, and Sharon had just shoved her foot smack in the center of the jagged hole. When she tried to lift it and correct her mistake, she only succeeded in catching the toe of her sneaker in Tim's exposed rib cage.

When the flashlight beam shifted to illuminate the gruesome scene, Jenny bellowed even louder from above – and the rest of the zombies sped up their progress toward the catwalk.

Great. Just fucking great.

With several zombies on the move – and too much experience watching horror flicks about murderous assailants and open staircases (like the one I was about to descend) – I decided not to wait for the inevitable to occur. Hugging the wall, I stuck the .38 in my holster and bolted down the steps. About five feet from Sharon, I pointed the shotgun at her head and pulled the trigger.

The subsequent blast turned the top half of her skull into an explosion of red mist, black ooze, and brain matter, and naturally, even more zombie gore landed on my skin and clothes. Tired of being covered in such foulness, I really regretted not grabbing a rain poncho before leaving Home Depot.

I hastened down the remaining stairs and stepped over the rancid, motionless bodies of Tim and Sharon. Beyond the cacophony of moans, groans, meows, and barks, I could no longer hear Jenny's bellowing. Not necessarily a good sign. Stiffening my back against the wall and shifting my focus toward the catwalk, I noticed she was pointing the flashlight down an aisle directly ahead of me. She might not have been the most reliable back-up shooter, but at least she hadn't abandoned me altogether.

Her silent signal gave me just enough time to lock eyes with the approaching zombie, swing the shotgun upward, and fire. Because the former male employee was at least six and a half feet tall – about eight inches taller than I was – my aim was slightly off. Instead of blasting his brains, the slug blew an enormous hole through his neck, severing his head from his body. Both dropped to the concrete floor, but while the body stopped twitching immediately, the head continued rolling toward the rear doors, which likely led into the storage area.

Jenny's flashlight beam pivoted toward a spot two aisles away. Gazing around to ensure she hadn't missed any closer zombies, I headed toward the place she'd indicated. Unfortunately, though, the blood-covered floor had become as slick as an ice-skating rink. My sneakers slipped, and I slid across the concrete, losing my grip on the shotgun in the process.

"Look out!" Jenny yelled, a bit too late to be helpful.

Sliding past my destination, I just missed colliding

into an overweight woman, sporting a fuzzy pink sweater covered in embroidered felines. Yep, an actual zombified cat lady grasped the air above my head as I sailed past her.

I crashed ungracefully into a cat litter display, righted myself as quickly as possible, and leaned against the pile of containers. After grabbing the .38 from my holster, I aimed the barrel at the cat lady and unloaded the remaining two shots. Luckily, I managed to hit her in the head twice, ending her flesh-eating days.

Since my .38 was now empty, the shotgun lay who-the-fuck-knew-where, and at least a couple zombies remained in the store, I didn't exactly love my odds of survival. At least the crowbar still hung from my belt.

Hastily, I shoved the .38 in my holster, but before I could rise to my feet, I heard a terrified caterwauling, followed by a shrill human scream. Although both sounds had come from the back of the sales floor, I instinctively glanced toward the catwalk. Jenny was no longer up there – and she wasn't on the stairs either.

A few seconds later, I heard half a dozen gunshots coming from the same place I'd heard the scream. While I'd been crashing into the litter containers and taking out the cat lady, Jenny had apparently darted across the catwalk, leapt down the stairs, and bolted along another aisle.

When I finally scrambled to my feet, I managed to find the Mossberg under a shelf in the next aisle. Quickly, I retrieved it and headed in Jenny's direction. Another half-dozen shots exploded in the store – basically, all of the bullets in the damn gun I'd lent her.

As I reached the cat food section, I discovered Jenny standing in the middle of the aisle, both arms extended, the empty 9mm still gripped in her hands. The flashlight rolled at her feet, where she'd likely dropped it, the beam illuminating a horrific scene several feet away. Two male zombies, their heads a mangled, bullet-riddled mess, lay on either side of a partially eaten feline, with a punctured bag of kibble in the distance.

"Holy crap, Jenny. What happened here?"

At the sound of my voice, she lowered the gun and turned to face me. Even with her puffy eyelids and tear-stained cheeks, I could see she no longer wore the expression of shock and dismay I'd seen upstairs. Her clenched jaws, flared nostrils, and steely eyes all pointed to one foregone conclusion: She was seething with anger.

"I saw movement off to the side. Realized Francis, the store's cat, had torn into a bag of kibble. He was probably starving, the poor thing. The two zombies were headed toward him. I tried to get to him in time, but they must've cornered him."

"Dammit," I said, taking a closer look at the eviscerated calico. "That's terrible."

"He had free reign over the place," she said, sniffling again. "People loved to visit with him. He was so sweet. And with all that's been happening around here, he was probably so scared and desperate. Much weaker than usual. An easy target."

"I'm really sorry," I told her with all sincerity, hoping Azazel was still safe in her carrier. "But we need to make sure there are no other zombies here."

Following a moment of renewed catatonia, she nodded in compliance. Then, once we'd reloaded our weapons with the bullets and shells I'd crammed into my pockets, we combed the rest of the store: up and down each aisle, across the bodies and debris, even in the adjacent rooms. Luckily, we only found three additional zombies: a man pinned beneath a pallet of dog food in the rear storage area, a boy wedged behind a vending machine in the employee break room, and a woman locked in the wheelchair-accessible stall in the ladies' restroom.

The first two had likely been trapped on purpose, but I suspected the woman, after receiving a bite on her forearm, had hidden in the bathroom, where she'd eventually turned. Sad as the situation was, we promptly put all three out of their misery.

Honestly, I was surprised we had found so few zombies in the Pet Mart. Given all the corpses and body parts we'd discovered, we knew several victims had endured too much brain trauma to reemerge as the undead. But still, I thought it would take us longer to secure the store. Perhaps some reanimated victims had wandered outside when the automatic doors still functioned.

After reloading our weapons again and ensuring no zombies remained, we checked on the cats and dogs that Jenny, her grandparents, and the other Humane Society volunteers had brought for the adoption event. Happily, all dozen of the remaining animals had endured their ordeal. Although blood and gore stained the area around the kennels, the zombies obviously hadn't figured out how to open the latches – and frankly, the animals seemed grateful to encounter people not trying to eat them.

Once we'd cleaned our hands and forearms with some hand sanitizer near the registers, we gave the cats and dogs some fresh water and kibble, then quickly checked the other critters in the store. The gerbils, hamsters, guinea pigs, rabbits, and turtles had all survived in their terrariums. Even the tropical fish – whose fish tanks were still powered, probably by a backup generator – had made it through the early stage of the zombie apocalypse. No less overjoyed than Jenny, I was also grateful our death-defying journey had been worth it.

Before returning to Home Depot, we decided to secure the adjacent shops and restaurants, too. As with similar complexes, a back corridor linked all the establishments. When we opened the door leading to it and illuminated the dark hallway with our trusty flashlight, I wasn't terribly surprised to find a couple zombies waiting for us.

Two Vietnamese cooks, each sporting bloody white aprons and ragged neck wounds, had apparently hidden from the madness in the rear corridor, only to succumb to their injuries. From the look of their decomposing, bloodless faces, I assumed they had yet to taste human flesh. Naturally, I had no intention of being their first meal as zombies.

After taking them out with two well-placed bullets, we cautiously checked all six establishments. While the Vietnamese restaurant and adjacent gaming store contained several zombified employees and customers, the two clothing shops – likely closed when the zombie attacks began – were devoid of the living or the dead. Same with two of the restaurants that were strictly breakfast and lunch joints.

Once we'd scouted and secured all six places, we returned to the Pet Mart, headed to the catwalk, and ventured toward the roof. No doubt Jenny's grandparents had heard all the gunshots and were still anxiously waiting for their granddaughter's safe return.

Chapter

29

"Don't ask me why I can't leave without my wife, and I won't ask you why you can." – David Dutton, *The Crazies* (2010)

When Jenny and I emerged from the dark stairwell into the afternoon sunlight, we had to give our eyes several seconds to adjust to the brightness. Sure enough, Alvin and Ellen were waiting on the opposite roof. As soon as they spotted their granddaughter, the tension visibly drained from their faces.

Several bulging plastic bags surrounded the old couple's feet. Apparently, while Jenny and I had been on our zombie-killing mission, her grandparents had ventured downstairs to gather some requisite cleaning supplies and water bottles for our next task: clean-up and sanitation.

Although eager to reach my wife, I didn't want to abandon the Summers clan just yet. So, after coaxing Ellen across the makeshift bridge, I left her with Jenny on the roof of the Pet Mart and assisted Alvin in lugging the supplies between buildings. Luckily, our recent ruckus had lured most of the zombies to the front of the pet store, dramatically reducing the size of our ravenous audience in the access road. Crossing the bridge was now significantly less distracting.

Once all four of us had safely reached the roof of the Pet Mart, we ventured downstairs to make the stores and restaurants more livable. While I didn't have time to help them tidy and sanitize every nook and cranny, I did lend a hand with two major tasks: clearing out a supply closet and hauling the corpses and body parts (even that of poor Francis) there for temporary storage.

By then, it was time for me to hit the road again. So,

the four of us crawled back across the bridge. Even Jenny made it without incident. Perhaps she was simply too exhausted to be scared.

Taking her earlier advice, I crept back into the van for some toiletries and a change of clothes and shoes, then tried to make myself presentable in the men's bathroom of Home Depot. Not easy without running water, but hand sanitizer, dry shampoo, deodorant, and mouthwash worked a bit of magic. I stuffed all my filthy items into a garbage bag and lugged it back to the contractor entrance, where the Summers family patiently awaited me.

Although Alvin seemed to have a solid plan for making use of the adjacent buildings and organizing the supplies we'd found during our clean-up duties, he needed just one more favor from me. So, after helping him with some necessary preparations, I was finally ready to leave.

Back in the van, I stowed my shotgun, bloody clothes, and supplies (including a couple ponchos I'd found on the floor of Home Depot). Then, I sprayed any areas I'd touched with either 409 or Febreze and hung the pine-scented air fresheners on the heating vents.

Near the contractor entrance, I gave the Summers clan some extra ammo and told them to keep the Beretta, derringer, extra shotgun, and flashlight. Yeah, I could've given them even more weapons, but frankly, I wanted to make sure Clare and I were well protected on our dangerous trek northward.

Luckily, the Summers family seemed to appreciate the guns – and all the assistance I'd offered them. So much so, in fact, they ended up parting with a couple rolls of duct tape from the cache of supplies they'd managed to assemble prior to the mass looting.

"I know you don't have time to fix your radiator yet," Alvin said, "but maybe this will help when you get where you're going."

I accepted the tape and heartily shook his hand. "Thanks, Al. I hope everything works out for you and your girls."

"No, thank *you*, Joe," Ellen said as she leaned forward to kiss my gore-free cheek. "We couldn't have done all that without you."

"Yes," Jenny agreed, pecking me on the opposite cheek. "Thanks for everything. Especially helping to save the animals."

In spite of my cantankerous ways, I was pleased to have aided the family. Frankly, part of me wanted to stay with the Summers clan a while longer. My headache had returned with a vengeance, and I could've used some sleep.

But my Home Depot stop had already delayed me longer than necessary – and I was no closer to repairing my busted radiator (or my dangling side-view mirror). Besides, I needed to do one last favor for Alvin – while he still had enough natural light to accomplish his task.

"Well, guys," I said, edging toward the glass doors, "I should hit the road. Good luck to the three of you."

"You, too," Jenny said. "I hope you find Clare."

"I will," I assured her. "That's not even a question."

She smiled sadly, and I turned away to avoid contemplating her expression.

After prying open the entrance one last time, I did a brief zombie check, unlocked the passenger-side door, and climbed past Azazel. I almost introduced her to the Summers family, but she'd already been rattled enough. Even though Alvin, Ellen, and Jenny adored animals, my cat had never been particularly friendly to strangers on a good day – much less a day where she'd endured multiple rollovers and innumerable zombie threats.

I set the crowbar and duct tape on the floor, not far from the Mossberg and my go-bag. Out of sheer habit, I made sure I'd slipped my wallet in the back pocket of my fresh jeans – not that credit cards and IDs mattered anymore. Then, I chased down a couple aspirin with a swig of warm soda, waved goodbye to the Summers clan, and watched them temporarily close the glass doors before shutting and locking my own door.

After buckling my seatbelt and starting the rumbling engine, which alerted quite a few zombies near Whole Foods, I blasted the heater and slowly drove away from Home Depot. As I plowed through any and all zombies in my diagonal path across the parking lot, I started blowing my loud-ass horn.

Part of my final favor to Alvin, the horn-blowing did exactly as expected: lured all the zombies away from the stores and restaurants. Of course, the hordes of undead were now following my van, as if it were some demented Pied Piper of New Orleans. Maybe it wasn't the safest plan, but I drove just fast enough to stay ahead of the stumbling creatures and avoid any other undead obstacles converging from elsewhere in the parking lot.

By the time I reached the street, it looked as though Azazel and I were leading a parade of costumed zombies in the Intergalactic Krewe of Chewbacchus. Only, the flesh-eaters behind my van were the real deal.

Carefully, I pulled onto Tulane Avenue, and instead of driving west as I'd originally planned, I turned right and headed back toward Broad. It would allow me a lengthier stretch to lure away the undead and check on my new friends' progress. With nearly all the zombies in the vicinity trailing my grotesque honking van, I suspected Jenny and her grandparents were temporarily in the clear.

Through my passenger-side window, I could see Jenny and Ellen prying open the doors with some tools of their own, then I watched as Alvin drove a forklift we'd found in the lumber section through the entrance. While the ladies kept watch, he haphazardly veered toward the propane tanks, lowered the lift, and scooped up an entire bank. After dumping his load inside, he returned for another bank of propane tanks.

When it was finally time for me to pick up speed and ditch the zombies, several of which had gotten dangerously close to my van, I realized the spry old man had made three back-to-back loading trips and managed to haul nearly a hundred propane tanks, plus one large refilling tank, into the store. Enough fuel to last the small family quite a long time.

With their task complete, Alvin, Ellen, and Jenny closed the doors and waved at me through the glass. Waving in return, I stepped on the gas and left the zombie horde in a cloud of exhaust. As I headed down Tulane, I glanced at

Azazel's carrier and noticed her green eyes watching me through the slits.

"Well, those were some nice folks back there," I said, my focus on the road again. "But it's a good thing they decided to stay behind. I don't think we could've fit the three of them, your mama, her mama, and all those animals in here after all."

Besides, Azazel never would've tolerated it. As far as she was concerned, there was only enough room for one furbaby. Believe me, Clare and I knew who called the shots in our own small family.

Chapter

30

"Plans are pointless. Staying alive is as good as it gets." – Selena, *28 Days Later...* (2002)

At the intersection of Tulane and South Broad, I turned right and headed southwest. A few blocks later, Broad passed under the I-10, the highway I'd almost gotten stuck on. Gazing upward, I felt grateful I hadn't continued to push my way along that route, which had literally become a parking lot.

Rather inconveniently, several zombies spotted me from the twenty-foot-high overpass and impulsively decided to belly-flop onto the van, just as I drove beneath them. Luckily, they all splatted on the pavement behind me, and though I doubted any of them had survived the fall, I certainly wasn't planning to stop and make sure. Besides, even if their skulls hadn't split open on the asphalt, their broken limbs would likely guarantee they wouldn't be able to chase me anytime soon.

Feeling pretty pleased with myself, I turned right onto Earhart Boulevard and immediately ran into a small traffic jam.

Shit. So much for my grand plan.

Apparently, numerous residents were still alive and attempting to flee the city. To make the situation worse, plenty of zombies wandered between the vehicles, slowing down our progress even more.

I glanced at the temperature gauge on my dashboard and grimaced. While the stop at Home Depot had taken much longer than intended, it had also allowed my radiator to cool down a little. Naturally, I still had to run the heater to keep the temperature in check, and though that little trick had worked since leaving the Summers clan, it definitely wasn't foolproof.

As I came to a screeching halt behind a line of cars and trucks and watched the temperature gauge steadily rise, I realized the van would still overheat if I didn't keep moving. Hell, if the motorists in front of me didn't move their asses, we'd likely all be eaten anyway.

When I could, I turned off Earhart and weaved my way through the pothole-riddled streets of a decimated industrial neighborhood. Since few motorists had opted for a similar detour, I only had to contend with an occasional pack of the undead.

I made several turns and seemed to get nowhere fast. Figuring we'd gone far enough to bypass the traffic jam, I decided to head back toward Earhart.

Not far from Xavier University, a predominantly black college, I passed a mob of about ten zombified students. Soon afterward, I spotted a group of white middle-class men and women huddled inside an open garage, dressed in business casual clothing and carrying suitcases. When they saw my vehicle, they darted toward the street, waving their arms and shouting.

"Please give us a ride," a blonde lady in her mid-thirties pleaded.

"We need to get out of here," a tall, dark-haired man in his early forties added.

While driving past them, I realized not a single one of them carried a weapon. Not a gun or a blade between them. Hell, none of those idiots even had a bat or a fucking golf club.

Glancing in the side-view mirror on my left, I watched the pack of zombies take notice of the fresh meat. I really didn't need to see another group of undead devour another bunch of desperate humans, like the ones outside Louis Armstrong Park. Darwin might've been right – evolution was all about survival of the fittest – but still, I wasn't a completely heartless asshole. Or at least I tried not to be.

"Fuck." I slammed on the brakes, unbuckled my seatbelt, and bolted to the back of the van. After securing the tarp over my arsenal, I opened the rear doors and beckoned toward the six people. "Get in," I ordered. "Quick!"

Still gripping their expensive-looking suitcases like their lives depended on it, the half-dozen idiots – three men and three women – jogged toward my van and clambered inside. When the last of them had tossed his luggage onto the floor and scrambled after it, I shut and locked the doors, just as the group of zombies reached us. Thumps resounded around the vehicle as the undead bodies tossed themselves against the back and side doors.

As the thuds and groans loudened, I hastened

between my six new passengers, some of whom had already made themselves comfortable on the sofa or at our dining table. Quickly, I reclaimed the driver's seat, stepped on the gas pedal, and sped down the street.

"Thank you, mister," a woman said.

"Yes, thank you," a few others echoed.

I had just turned onto Calliope Street, planning to use South Jefferson Davis Parkway as a shortcut back to Earhart, when the tall, dark-haired man stepped between the front seats, gazed at Azazel's carrier, and grasped the seatbelt. Before he could unbuckle her, she hissed at him.

"No," I said, "the carrier stays there. She's all strapped in and sleeping."

Azazel hissed at him again, both to underscore and undermine my point.

The man shot me a disgruntled look but released the seatbelt. His displeasure only deepened when I hit a particularly large pothole and he nearly lost his grip on the seat.

I kept one hand on the steering wheel as I buckled my own seatbelt. "Hey, why don't you sit back there? Could get too bumpy to stand."

Balancing himself against the seat, he shot me one more nasty look before taking my advice and returning to his friends.

As I turned right onto Jefferson Davis, I slowed down and glanced over my shoulder at the expectant faces staring at me. "My name is Joe."

Most of them nodded or said "hello," but none of them introduced themselves.

Checking the road ahead, I asked, "Why don't you all have any weapons?" I glanced back at my inconvenient passengers. "Don't you know what's going on?"

"We were supposed to be picked up by the National Guard, but they never showed up," a balding red-haired man explained in a nasally voice.

I shot him a *so-fucking-what* look, then faced forward again. "You should all still have weapons. Just in case."

"I don't own a gun," one of the women said. "None of us do."

"Doesn't have to be guns," I replied. "Even a crowbar would be helpful against a hungry zombie."

While I'd initially thought each of my new passengers had a profound death wish, I realized the truth was much simpler: They were just clueless. Well-to-do types, either residents from a fancy Uptown neighborhood or executives in town for a convention. Either way, they were probably the least prepared – or least resourceful – people I'd encountered so far, and I wondered how the hell they'd survived for so long.

"Well, listen," I said, turning onto Earhart, "I'm heading to Baton Rouge. I can take you all as far as that."

An uncomfortable silence greeted my offer. Glancing over my shoulder, I noticed a few of them exchanging frowns and arched eyebrows.

Now, what?

Before I lost my patience, I decided to ignore them for a while and just continue driving down Earhart, swerving around bodies, zombies, and stalled cars whenever necessary. Eventually, I planned to merge onto South Clearview Parkway and turn onto Airline Drive, which would ultimately become Airline Highway and hopefully guide me all the way to Baton Rouge – and to Clare.

Chapter

31

"Good. Bad. I'm the guy with the gun." – Ash, *Army of Darkness* (1992)

A few minutes later, I heard murmurs behind me. My passengers had begun talking amongst themselves, quietly enough that, with my compromised hearing, I couldn't understand their words. Clearly, they didn't want me to understand.

I gazed down at my hip holster. Wisely, I'd checked

the .38 before leaving Home Depot – just to ensure it was fully loaded. Since my passengers weren't likewise armed, I wasn't exactly worried. Just annoyed.

"Jesus," one of the women suddenly said. "Why's it so hot in here? Do you have the heater on?"

"I'm having radiator problems," I explained without turning around. "The heat helps to keep the temps down."

"Well, can you turn it off?" one of the guys asked. "Maybe turn the A/C on instead?"

"I *said*," I insisted, "the radiator is having some trouble. The heat needs to stay on. Sorry."

Can't believe I just apologized to these asshats.

"Listen," another guy interjected, "maybe we need to talk about where we're headed."

"What?" Had I heard him right?

"Yeah," one of the women added, "maybe we should vote on where we should go."

"I'm going to Baton Rouge," I repeated.

My van. My decision. Piss off if you don't like it.

"That's not right," another woman protested. "There

are seven of us in here. We should all have a say."

What the holy fuck is going on? What's wrong with these people?

I had kindly welcomed them into my van, just moments before they would've become zombie food, and that was how they repaid me: by staging a mutiny?

As far as I was concerned, even Azazel's opinion counted more than whatever those pricks wanted – and I was positive that, if she could've spoken English, she would've ordered me to keep heading toward the state capital. Where her beloved mama was.

"Yeah, we should turn around and head east," the whiny redhead stated. "We heard Baton Rouge was almost as bad as New Orleans."

"Look," I said through gritted teeth, "I'm going to get my wife in Baton Rouge. You can either ride there with me, or I can let you out now."

"No, we should drive to the East Coast," the redhead repeated.

That's it. I've had enough of this bullshit.

Slowly, I unbuckled my seatbelt and, reaching downward, pulled a towel-covered bundle from beneath my seat. While still navigating my way down Earhart, I carefully unrolled the towel, slid the contents of the bundle into my lap, and leaned sideways to cover Azazel's carrier.

"Yeah, we have friends in Savannah," another man said. "Joyce and I think that's where we should go."

Murmurs of agreement followed his proposal.

"Yes," a woman, presumably Joyce, concurred. "Savannah is the perfect choice. Our friends have an enormous house by the coast."

"Uh, Joe, is it?" *Ugh.* The whiny redhead again. "Could you turn around? We need to take I-10 East."

Glancing over my shoulder, I noticed all three of the guys had risen to their feet and were slowly approaching me.

So, that's how it's gonna be? After I saved your fucking lives?

I kept driving and gazed down at my lap.

From the dining table, one of the women must've been watching me. "What's that?" she asked.

"A gas mask," I replied, calmly pulling it over my face.

Then, before anyone could react, I slammed on the

brakes, stopping my vehicle in the middle of the westbound lanes of Earhart Expressway. The three men tumbled onto the floor, and the women yelped.

I held out my right hand. With my left, I yanked the pin from the tear gas grenade and dropped both onto the floor behind my seat.

"Get the fuck outta my van!" Just in case that wasn't persuasive enough, I pulled my .38 from its holster and faced my flabbergasted passengers.

As the gas quickly filled up the van, I made sure the towel was tucked tightly beneath the edges of Azazel's carrier. The next instant, my new passengers' confusion morphed into horror. Screaming in pain, they hastily stumbled toward the rear doors. Some still gripped their suitcases, others had left them behind, but all of them wanted off the ride.

With undoubtedly stinging eyes, the dark-haired man fumbled with the locks for what seemed like forever, then he pushed open the doors and tumbled into the street. His compatriots swiftly followed, still shouting and crying and cursing my name.

As soon as the last woman dropped out, I put my foot on the gas and rolled about fifty feet forward before stopping again. I walked toward the rear of the van and turned on the high-capacity fan I'd mounted to the ceiling. Figured it would help to dissipate the gas and blow it out of my vehicle. Meanwhile, I tossed the remaining suitcases onto the road, kicked the tear gas canister outside, and, still wearing the gas mask, observed the assholes I'd just unceremoniously gassed and dumped into the street.

In theory, Clare wouldn't have approved of what I'd done, but if she'd realized just how close I'd probably come to losing our vehicle – and perhaps Azazel, too – she might've reconsidered.

As for me, I simply couldn't muster sympathy for the six ingrates coughing in agony on the asphalt, clutching their faces and rubbing their eyes. They'd accepted my charity without question and all but spit in my face. Sooner or later, selfish people like them would get others killed. In the end, maybe I'd done a service for my fellow survivors.

For a moment, I stood in the doorway, not really rationalizing my actions...

Cuz fuck them.

Then, as I pulled one door shut, I noticed a figure step into the street, about thirty feet behind the van. It wasn't a zombie, at least not like all the others I'd seen. For one thing, it seemed to walk with purpose.

Abruptly, it stopped, turned its head, and stared at me. I couldn't help but scan its features; my curiosity was just too overwhelming.

Even through my gas mask, I could tell it wore ragged pants, with no shoes or shirt. It had well-defined muscles – and sparse patches of hair on its body. Incredibly, it showed no signs of decomposition whatsoever.

Strangely, its hands featured long nails, as if they hadn't been cut in years. Really, they seemed to resemble claws.

As we continued to gaze at each other, I realized that, unlike the zombies I'd encountered all day, the creature appeared to possess some measure of intelligence. While I'd been assessing it, its eyes had been surveying me, too, as if its brain was trying to process what it had just witnessed.

It definitely wasn't a zombie, but I wasn't sure it was fully human either.

Whatever the fuck it was, I needed to get out of there. I just had to keep moving forward.

Turning away from me, the creature headed toward the huddle of my former passengers as they continued to cry and cough. While locking the rear doors, I saw it close the gap by leaping the last ten feet and bowling into the group.

Heartless as it might sound, I didn't intend to watch the carnage about to occur.

A moment later, I'd returned to the driver's seat, laid the mask on the floor, and removed the towel from Azazel's carrier. She gazed at me with moist, red-rimmed eyes and meowed sadly. Despite my precautions, the tear gas had obviously seeped into her carrier.

"I'm sorry," I said, opening the gate. "I know you don't understand why your eyes are stinging, but I promise it's for a good reason. Your daddy had to protect you from a bunch of selfish fucktards."

Slowly, she emerged from the carrier, hopped onto the floor, and stretched her legs.

"No matter what, though, I think you've earned a walkabout."

While Azazel made a beeline for her litter box, I shifted the van into drive and stepped on the gas. Back on track again, I breathed a little easier.

Well, shit.

I suddenly remembered I'd forgotten to put Clare's ring back in her jewelry box. Once again stopping, I felt my pocket for the round outline... but it wasn't there.

"Fuck." A sense of panic gripped my innards. "Where the hell is it?"

As the frustration mounted, I abruptly recalled my brief cleanup in the Home Depot restroom. Frantically, I searched through the bag of dirty duds – and exhaled an enormous sigh of relief when I located the ring. After sanitizing both it and my hands, I tucked the ring into my pocket and reclaimed the driver's seat.

So glad I didn't burn my jeans, like Jenny suggested.

What a nightmare if I'd lost my wife's ring somewhere during the day's surreal adventures... if it had slipped out of my pants when I'd tumbled in Home Depot or crawled across the makeshift bridge or crashed into the cat litter display inside the Pet Mart. No way in hell I'd return to the city, but still, I'd have felt like a real jackass for risking my life for the damn thing in the first place.

Luckily, though, I didn't have to fixate on that. I just needed to keep my eyes on the road and focus on seeing Clare again.

And fuck if I'll be picking up any more strangers.

My altruistic vein had just run dry.

Emerging from her litter box, Azazel looked up at me. A single tear dribbled down her furry cheek. The tear certainly wasn't for the idiots we'd just dumped on the road. I didn't feel bad for them, and I doubted she did either. I did, however, feel guilty that, even with the towel over her carrier, she'd unfortunately suffered a bit from the gas. After the harrowing day we'd had, I owed her some tuna. A whole helluva lot.

"It's alright, girl. Those people sucked ass."

I didn't know what that creature was I'd just seen, but I knew I didn't want to mess with it. It was time to get the fuck out of New Orleans. I simply needed to get to Clare and keep heading north.

Even over the rumbling engine, I heard a loud screech from behind us. Gazing at my side-view mirror, I realized not one of the assholes was moving. Worse, the figure stood nearby, staring at us.

A few seconds later, it had vanished.

Fuck this.

I hit the gas and continued down the expressway, hoping nothing and no one delayed me from reaching my wife. After the fucking horrific day I'd had, even my mother-in-law would be a welcome sight.

Well, not sure I'd go that far. But who knows? Stranger things have certainly happened.

Survive the Zombie Chaos

CONTINUE THE CHAOS

Highway to Hell: Zombie Chaos Book 2

Out of the frying pan... into the fires of zombie hell!

Getting out of undead-infested New Orleans was only the first step. With my cat, Azazel, in tow, I have to trek nearly eighty miles to Baton Rouge, where I hope to find my wife, Clare, still alive.

But these days, the road to good intentions is soaked with blood, brains, and zombie foulness. After all, the Big Easy outbreak isn't an isolated incident, and I have to drive the ol' zombie-mobile through an assortment of highways and byways crawling with the undead. Of course, it might be the living that pose the greatest threat. Gotta love humanity... Not.

Highway to Hell is the second book in the *Zombie Chaos* series, a post-apocalyptic tale filled with graphic language, graphic gore, and, naturally, graphic snark.

Not already a zombie? That's awesome! Stay alive and join us by becoming a Survivor (http://zombiechaos.com/become-a-survivor).

We know you love your freedom, so we promise not to bombard you with junk mail. We'll only notify you about new releases, giveaways, and recommendations.

If you enjoyed *Escape from the Big Easy: Zombie Chaos Book 1*, please consider leaving a positive review.

About the Authors

D.L. Martone is the joint pen name of husband-wife duo Daniel and Laura Martone. Part-time residents of New Orleans and northern Michigan, the Martones travel the country in their mobile writing studio, a cozy RV dubbed *Serenity*. As you might have guessed, they're huge fans of *Firefly*, which is why they remodeled the interior of their travel trailer to resemble Captain Reynolds' beloved spaceship. Together, they enjoy writing space opera, fantasy game lit, urban fantasy, time travel, cozy mysteries, and, of course, post-apocalyptic zombie tales.

Acknowledgments

We appreciate the support from our friends, families, and fellow writers – and the inspiration gleaned from various zombie flicks and TV shows, especially *Shaun of the Dead*, *The Walking Dead*, and George Romero's *Dead* movies – as well as our fellow fans of such stories.

Of course, we couldn't have started this series – or finished this book – without the love and support of each other and our beloved kitty, Ruby Azazel.

Lastly, we're grateful to you, our fellow survivors, for joining Joe on his harrowing journey through zombie-filled New Orleans and beyond.

Made in the USA
Las Vegas, NV
14 January 2021

15856022R00173